TIME OUT

stories from Punjab

TIME OUT

stories from Punjab

Foreword by
K.S Duggal

Editor
Jasjit Mansingh

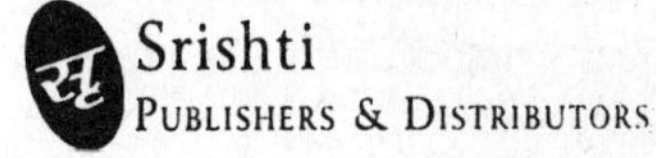
Srishti
Publishers & Distributors

SRISHTI PUBLISHERS & DISTRIBUTORS
64-A, Adhchini
Sri Aurobindo Marg
New Delhi 110 017
srishtipublishers@yahoo.com

First published in 2002 by SRISHTI PUBLISHERS & DISTRIBUTORS
Second printing, 2004

ISBN 81-87075-90-2
Rs. 195.00

Typeset in AGaramond 11pt. by Suresh Kumar Sharma at Srishti

Cover Illustration: *Earthen Pot* by Arpana Caur
Cover Design by Arrt Creations
45 Nehru Apartment, Kalkaji, New Delhi 110 019
arrt@vsnl.com

Printed and bound in India

CONTENTS

I

III

FOREWORD

K S Duggal

The short story is considered to be the most popular form of writing in modern literature. It has greater appeal because it portrays the thoughts and emotions of common people. For the reader the short story not only represents life but is considerate to the reader because of the contemporary lack of leisure. The art of the short story lends itself well to the subjective and impressionistic rather than to the merely realistic or judgemental. It is a flexible form of writing which can accommodate the philosophy of serious thinkers or the confusion of the moderns. It can be dramatic, lyrical, or imbued with irony and pathos. It can reflect the troubled times we live in and function as social commentary.

In modern times, when falsehood and lies are accepted as the norm specially in politics, as though the vehicle of life cannot move without lies, it becomes the business of the story writer to grope in the heaps of garbage and pull out the truth of life in all its grossness, filter it through his own prism and give it presentable shape. In our country, the voice of the Bengali writer is heard, the Marathi writer cannot be ignored, and Malayali writers lead their society at every step, but Punjabi writers have not been so well-known in English. In recent decades the tide has turned and there is a renaissance in Punjabi literature. It gives me great pleasure to see this collection of short stories featuring some of our great writers. It gives me even greater pleasure to know that these stories have been brought to the English-reading public for the first time.

The modern writer of Punjab has had cause to shed tears of blood and question society and the government about the innocent deaths of the people of Punjab in the decade 1984-94. A recent publication puts the number of people killed – men, women, and children – at 25,000. Many more died in the wars with Pakistan, and hardly any of them was guilty. They were mostly innocent citizens including those who had come to a prosperous Punjab from Bihar in search of a livelihood. I am glad to see some of the stories in the middle section of the book deal with such realities which have scarred the psyche of a generation deeply. The flames of communal divisiveness were fanned for partisan and political ends but despite that a basic humanism emerges cutting through the barriers of the religious divide in the best tradition of Guru Nanak.

Many writers in the last decades of the century have been involved with such questions including myself. I hope that some more of them, for example Prem Gorkhi, Waryam Sandhu, Pritam Siddhu, Gurbachan Singh Bhullar or Darshan Mitwa, will find a place in the second volume in this series.

The voice of the Punjabi writer needs to be heard again as it was at the time of Partition. I particularly compliment the editor on including *Kis da Katal* by Tauquir Chugtai, who writes in Punjabi from Pakistan, and speaks powerfully for sanity through the undivided subcontinent in a world gone mad with hate. He invokes the Buddha as the unifying force of love and compassion through two-and-a-half millenia of time, and space which reaches far beyond the mountain fastness of Bamiyan.

K S Duggal

New Delhi
15 December 2001

EDITOR'S NOTE

I have the honour to present this collection of short stories from the Punjab and acknowledge with deep gratitude the help rendered by Sardar Pritam Singh of Navyug Press, the leading publisher of Punjabi literature affectionately known as Bhapaji, in selecting them. I am also grateful to Mr K S Duggal, scholar and litterateur, for his suggestion that it would be a greater service to the language to chose for this anthology stories not previously translated. That effectively ruled out most of his own work. The exception was "Jogian de kanaan vich kach diyan mundran", (The Tantrik's Promise), a long short story and the only one not translated into English. Regretfully, I abandoned the highly acclaimed "The Night of the Full Moon", which won the Sahitya Akademi Award, translated brilliantly by Khushwant Singh and available to the English reader in many other anthologies.

In the initial selection I had deliberately avoided including any of the bloodcurdling stories spawned by the most traumatic event in India's history during the twentieth century – the Partition of Punjab and Bengal. The transfer of power to the new states of India and Pakistan was based on the principle of a dominant religion. But when 11 September 2001 happened, it was no longer possible to turn a blind eye to any form of bigotry.

Terror, bloodshed, rape, barbarity are the underlying themes of many of the stories set in the context of five thousand years of the history of Indian civilisation. Yet there is often a counterpoint of ordinary human decency, of goodness. The geographic region known as Punjab has been a frontline state. It has borne the brunt of all, including the Muslim, overland invasions over a period of many hundred years. In more recent times fresh wounds have been inflicted on the psyche of the Punjabi, whether Hindu, Sikh or Muslim, which will take a long time to heal. Terrorism provides the underpinning, cutting across the rural-urban and the rich-poor divide in such stories as "Splintered" by Raj Gill or "He is not that Jasbir" by Prem Prakash. Ajeet Cour's powerful indictment of a corrupt society, "November 1984," cannot be ignored in an anthology of writing from Punjab. I am grateful to her for suggesting it and also her other story included here, a diametrically opposite and charming tale of hope not entirely lost, "On Vacation".

Baldev Singh's, "Her Last Cries," and the eminent Pakistani writer, Tauquir Chugtai's "Who did they Murder?" are only fifty years apart in time and what different worlds they depict! I have to thank Amrita Pritam for bringing both to my notice. As for her own stories, she kindly offered me five untranslated stories to chose from and suggested these two as her favourites: "Bhabi Morni" and "And the River Kept Flowing...".

The theme of mother-love and the power of Shakti, the Feminine Principle in its various forms, runs through the stories in the first section. In "The Tantrik's Promise" it is the power of passionate love and the length to which it drives a woman. Kulwant Singh Virk is represented by two short stories written in a classic style – pithy and poignant. Buta Singh, in "Sardarni" builds his story of rivalry and intrigue around the central matriarchal figure who dominates a joint family and seeks to assert her will on the extended family of in-laws. Told so deftly, we don't know whether to laugh or cry.

Manmohan Bawa's canvas is wider and his exploration of the depth's of a woman's feelings and conflicting loyalties exquisite. I thank him for the help he gave in explaining some obscure dialect terms which had baffled my mother. I am grateful also for the pen and ink sketches he did specially for this book.

A word about the translations. My name appears alone against some of the translations, but I could not have done them without my mother, Mrs Devinder Kaur Assa Singh's help and her intimate knowledge of the Punjabi ethos and literature. She didn't consider her help substantial enough to allow me to use her name except in two stories. It was she who vetted the short stories, often in agreement with Sardar Pritam Singh. Her only limitation is failing eyesight and hearing but considering the fact that she was born in 1906 that is to be expected. I would need to mark passages and words, hand her her glasses and her magnifying glass – either in the morning or afternoon when there was sufficient natural light – and she would read and explain. I would then hone the final draft and give her a printout to do a final crosscheck. She has a doctorate in psychology (from the University of London in 1931) and her interpretation of the bear in Baldev Singh's story, "Her Last Cries", had escaped both Tara and me. It is not explicit in the story and I will allow the reader to decide. Together we won the first all India translation award from Katha for Punjabi for Ajeet Cour's "Yudhishter."

Tara, a Tamil brahmin who married a Punjabi and lived in Punjab, is a graduate in Sanskrit and speaks Tamil, Hindi, Urdu and Punjabi fluently. She has worked closely with Amrita Pritam and translated her work in *Fifty Fragments of Inner Self* published by Hind Books. She has a post-M A diploma in Linguistics from Delhi University.

Satjit Wadva, part-Grewal as is my mother, had a traditional upbringing in Punjab. She taught at Guru Harkrishan Public School, New Delhi, for two decades and has translated the works of Osho and other metaphysical writing besides "Aa Behn Fatima", an award-winning story for Katha.

The responsibility for editing all the stories is mine. The usual balancing act has been performed between being true to the original story yet allowing it to flow in English without pulling the reader up short to the fact of it being a translation. Once again I need to thank Janaki Kathpalia for her eagle eye and for spotting whatever escaped me in the final proof. Janaki, another Tamil brahmin, and Tara both suggest that a glossary would make it easier for the non-Hindi/Punjabi reader specially for the kinship terms used in many of the stories. As an example she said she knew what a 'khes' was only after she married her Punjabi husband. I believe, however, that the meanings will be evident in the context for the imaginative reader.

The arrangement of the stories will allow the reader to get a sense of the layers of time and events which went into the makeup of the modern Punjabi. Our roots are not easy to escape.

"Hunger" by Kishen Singh Dhody is reproduced from the anthology published by Jaico some years ago. It was first published in *The Illustrated Weekly* in the 1960s, translated by Khushwant Singh. It came my way fortuitiously and I couldn't ignore the circumstances which brought it to my notice. As far as I am aware, it is the only story in this collection which has been published in English before.

I

UDAMBARA

Manmohan Bawa

When Jaidev completed his studies, in five years, with Acharya Kalyan Mitra, Kalyani, the Acharya's daughter had blossomed into womanhood. Of all the students in the Ashram, Jaidev was the most intelligent and hard working. His memory was phenomenal. He had to listen only once to be able to remember word by word.

Whenever Kalyani happened to pass by none of the students could refrain from stealing a glance at her. It was as though her limbs were impatient to be free from the restraint of her clothes. There was a gleam in her eyes and on her lips a smile full of joy. That is none except Jaidev. Never did her beauty, or the tinkle of her anklets, distract him from his single-minded concentration.

His education complete, when Jaidev was preparing to go home to Roop Nagar (today's Ropar in Punjab), Acharya Kalyan Mitra, according to the tradition of those days, arranged the

---

Translated by Devinder Kaur Assa Singh and Jasjit Mansingh

marriage of his daughter Kalyani with his first and foremost pupil Jaidev. They were expected to leave together. Kalyani and Jaidev spent one night with each other in the same room. Kalyani sat on the bed and waited, a long time, for him. When he came he spread a mat on the floor and, turning his back towards Kalyani, lay down. Shyly she went to sit next to him on the mat but he got up and moved to the bed. That is how the night passed.

Kalyani thought to herself: May be he is shy, or perhaps he doesn't know what a marital relationship should be.... Well, never mind! This brahmachari will come to know in a few days.... And thinking about the days to come she giggled silently.

The next day, walking alongside Jaidev, Kalyani wondered about him: What a strange man he is! Can't he feel the heat of the fire leaping out from my body? Is he not attracted to my sparkling eyes, or by my lips as sweet as honey? Walking on this path through the forest does he get no messages from the twittering of the birds and the presence of pairs of lovelorn deer? This stupid fellow keeps walking along, in silence, utterly oblivious of my presence...! Well! Let the night come! I will see how much control he has over himself!

By sunset they reached the banks of the river Purusini, also known as Ravi, and stopped. A boat was tied to a tree but there was no boatman in sight. Perhaps he had gone home.

They collected some wood, lit a fire and sat around it. Having eaten the chapatis they had brought with them from home, Kalyani stretched raising her arms upwards and as she did so the knot at the back of her choli opened, or perhaps she had already deliberately loosened it. She did not try to cover herself and, looking at Jaidev with eyes intoxicated with desire, she went and sat close to him, her body touching his. Jaidev jumped up and moved away to stand at a safe distance.

Kalyani's eyes blazed with anger and, looking like a wounded lioness, she cried out: "Doesn't the sight of my body, my rounded legs and arms, attract you at all? Can't you see that my feminity is calling out to your own masculinity...?"

Jaidev felt a stirring within him, a quickening, like the waves of a river in flood. But he controlled himself and spoke in a calm voice.

"Forgive me Devi Kalyani. You are the daughter of my most revered teacher and Guru. And...."

"The Guru's daughter!" She cut him short and continued vehemently: "Am I not your wife? If...If..." and she fell silent.

"Sit down, Kalyani, and let me also sit. I am very tired." Then, after a while, Jaidev continued. "I have no answer to your questions Kalyani except that I am not good enough to be your husband. I said the same thing to Guruji but he paid no attention. In reality I am not what you see. I have no background, nor any future. I can only say that there is still time. We have done nothing yet. You should go back home...."

He continued in the same vein for a long time, making no sense. Kalyani couldn't make out what he was trying to say. She was also feeling very tired, having walked the whole day and also because of her mental confusion. She put her head on her knees and had no idea when she slipped into sleep.

In the morning when she opened her eyes she saw she had

been covered with a brownish blanket. Jaidev was not there, nor was the boat that had been moored on the bank.

Raja Vishnu Varman was hunting in the forest accompanied by some of his soldiers and was quite surprised to see a pretty girl perched in the fig tree growing by the river bank. She was busy eating figs. On seeing the Raja she climbed down.

"Who are you?" the Raja asked. "And what are you doing in the forest all by yourself?"

She looked at the Raja and then at the guards. She thought for a while and then answered. "You won't believe what I say, so just think that I am alone in this world. There is nobody in my past, nor will there be in the future.

'What do I need to know about your past... or future,' thought the Raja impressed by her beauty. And he asked, "Would you like to come with me?"

"There is no point in asking her," one of his companions proffered sensing the Raja's attraction. "According to the scriptures anything that does not belong to anybody is the Raja's property."

"What is your name?" the Raja asked.

"I want to forget my past, everything about myself, even my name."

"Good. I found you sitting on the udambar tree ... I will call you Udambara.

For a few days Udambara lived in the Raja's harem. But with her beauty, intelligence and knowledge of the scriptures

Udambara soon became the Raja's favourite queen. People were impressed when she quoted from the shastras and vedas which she had imbibed through living with her learned father. The Raja slipped into the habit of confiding in her and consulting her on various problems of state.

One day when the Raja and Udambara were returning from a walk by the banks of the river Satadru (Sutlej) a brahmin appeared on the path before them, his hands folded in a respectful greeting. Upon being asked, he said:

"I am a poor brahmin. I have heard that your scribe has passed away. If in that position I can be of service to you I will consider myself very fortunate."

"You have heard correctly. But I need an experienced and efficient person."

"Don't judge me by my youthful appearance, Rajan. You will see that I have asked for far less than my capability."

Udambara found the voice of the brahmin familiar. She turned to look and saw that it was none other than Jaidev, her husband. Momentarily their eyes met and he bowed his head respectfully and lowered his gaze. She felt that he had not recognised her but she herself had no doubts at all.

Instantly there flashed in her mind the memory of the night they had spent on the banks of the Purusini. Overcoming a rising wave of anger she asked in a detached voice:

"Have you worked anywhere or is all your learning from books?" Her heart was racing, she was impatient to know whether he *had* recognised her.

Seeing that he hadn't, anger overcame her. How could he not? How could he be so careless, so unaware of her? Perhaps he had never really looked at her. She would have her revenge!

"I have transcribed texts of the shastras in the library of Patliputra. And for sometime I was in the service of the Raja of Tregarta (Kangra)."

She looked at the Raja who understood what she wanted, and he said to Jaidev, "Hmmm. Present yourself tomorrow. We will see how capable you are."

Udambara was mistaken when she thought that Jaidev had not recognised her. He had come to this kingdom only because he had heard she was here. He was pleased that she was mistaken and also that she had recognised him.

After wandering aimlessly for three or four years he had an intense desire to see Kalyani and to know what had become of her. He had become worldly wise perhaps because he had suffered at the hands of Brahmins at two or three places. This time he had no clear plan except the conviction that 'Rani' Udambara was his wedded wife who had once loved him with a pure heart. He thought that even if the outcome of his visit should not be happy, neither could harm come of it.

Six months passed.

Jaidev had joined as a humble scribe and he remained one. He made no progress. Nor did the Raja take any special interest in him. He had only a small two-roomed house to live in.

There were a few occasions during these six months that Jaidev and Udambara happened to be alone together but he made no effort to lay any claim to her. Udambara, on the other hand, willed him to make a move. At night she would lie in bed and think about him and her body would be inflamed with desire.

'No. No!' She would admonish herself. 'I must not think like this. I am now the queen and it is essential for the sake of my own honour and prestige that this distance, this non-recognition remain as it is.' At the same time, every day she could not help herself feeling frustrated and angry with him. And an impatience to know that reason, the reason why Jaidev ran away leaving her alone in the forest.

One morning, when Jaidev was returning from the river after his bath people heard the cries of a woman coming from a secluded part of the forest. When they went there, they found the maid Kanchanmala, her clothes torn, screaming and shouting that Jaidev had tried to take advantage of her....

The matter was brought before Raja Vishnu Varman.

Udambara was both indignant and angry: "He tried to molest my maid! He should be severely punished.... He deserves to be flogged...."

The Raja felt that Jaidev and Kanchanmala ought to be questioned separately to establish what had happened. Who knows it might be something entirely different. Even if it should be true, he should be removed from his post and it should be enough to have him leave the country. A brahmin is a learned man. It is not right that he should be flogged.

Udambara panicked. If the truth were to become known it

would surely back-fire!

The Raja called Jaidev and asked him: "Is it true what we have heard?"

Jaidev looked penetratingly at Udambara who was standing close by. This time there was recognition in his eyes and also a question. He then turned to the Raja and said:

"I am a poor brahmin and she is the Rani's maid. Therefore what she says must be right."

"Is it or isn't it right? Speak clearly."

"How can he speak clearly!" Udambara said as she looked at Jaidev sharply and continued. "I know men like him very well. He is now playing the innocent! Who knows how many times this brahmin has played with the lives of others."

Jaidev stood quietly.

"You have two options," the Raja said thoughtfully. "To leave my kingdom or be flogged."

"Men commit many mistakes unintentionally," he said speaking more for Udambara's benefit than to the Raja. "There are certain compulsions which dictate a man's actions, or perhaps there are other reasons.... Sometimes he is simply unable to distinguish between right and wrong. If I am forgiven after the lashing I consider myself fortunate."

The Raja, looking towards Udambara and then towards Kanchanmala who was standing behind the door, said: "All right. As you wish."

Astonished, Kanchanmala wondered: 'Why is the Rani behaving like this. Why is she so against this poor brahmin? And why is he putting up with it without protest? What is going on…?'

When the soldiers were taking him away, Kanchanmala plucked up courage and whispered to them: "The Raja orders that you use restraint. He should not be grievously hurt…." Perhaps Raja Vishnu Varman had the same thought in his mind.

One day when the Raja had gone hunting Udambara sent a message to Jaidev by hand of Kanchanmala summoning him.

When Jaidev came she spoke to him: "I wish to send a message to a man, the man who left me in the darkness of the night on the banks of the river Purusini and went away."

Looking directly into Udambara's eyes for the first time, Jaidev said: "If you have already recognised the man what is the need for all this play acting?"

"You are the one who has been pretending, since you too had recognised me. My only fault is that I did not wish to expose you and thus put you in a dilemma."

"And what is your excuse today?"

"All I want to know is why you left me in the forest and went away. Was I a cripple? Or ugly? Was I not the daughter of a highly respected family?"

"Don't be angry, Kalyani…."

"Kalyani!" Udambara expostulated. "So you remember my name?"

"I remember everything. Also that you are the daughter of a learned brahmin. It is precisely because of this that I left you and went away."

"For this reason? I don't understand."

"The truth is that that evening too I was putting on an act. I don't know if you will be able to forgive me if I tell you the real reason."

"Tell me clearly and don't try to be so smart."

"The truth is, Kalyani, that I am not a brahmin. I am only the son of a poor shudra."

Kalyani's jaw dropped and she gazed at him in wide-eyed astonishment. Jaidev continued:

"My father was a boatman. When I was born and when I grew up people remarked on my appearance and my intelligence: 'If he had been born to a kshatriya or brahmin household.... Surely there must be some kshatriya or brahmin among his ancestors...!'

"You see, when I was about fourteen or fifteen there was a small incident. Such incidents happen quite frequently among low caste people. That day my father had made many trips across the river Satadru. He was quite exhausted. My mother had been waiting for him to come and eat. He had only finished half his meal when five or six high caste people arrived at the riverbank. There was one brahmin among them and the rest were kshatriyas. They seemed to be in a great hurry. As soon as they reached they said imperiously to my father:

'Get up and take us across the river immediately.'

'Let me finish my food and I'll take you,' my father said.

'You can have your food later. We are in a hurry,' another scolded my father.

"My father got frightened. He left his food unfinished. He

quickly washed his hands in the river and as he waved them to dry perhaps a few drops of water fell on the brahmin. Angrily, the brahmin spoke: 'This low caste has defiled me! I will have to bathe and we will be delayed....' The kshatriyas beat up my father. They might even have beaten him to death if it were not for the fact that they needed to cross the river."

"Then...?" asked Udambara.

"I don't know what was going on in my father's mind. Or how often such things may have happened to him. Controlling his anger he picked up the oars. He looked balefully at the six of them as they got into the boat and he then started rowing. Once or twice he looked towards us as though he wanted to say something. When the boat reached exactly mid-stream, we saw it was rocking violently and suddenly it turned upside down. Those six, and my father – all seven of them – drowned."

"Your father too?" Udambara asked her mind working overtime.

"My father was a good swimmer. But one of those six could also swim. When he struck out my father caught up with him.... He wasn't going to allow him to get away, and the two of them also drowned."

Udambara sat silently for a while. It seemed as though she had been deeply affected by this incident. Jaidev continued.

"Thank God no one else witnessed this or else both of us would have had to suffer for it.... There is nothing remarkable if a boatman dies in the water or if a soldier dies on the battlefield. After the few days of weeping and crying when I took charge of the trade, my mother called me and said: 'Listen, Son. I don't want that you too should spend your life like a draught animal. You are not a fool like us. You are intelligent. Go to a good acharya and learn. I hear there is a place across the Purusini where they don't pay so much attention to caste.' She then sold herself to some wealthy merchant and gave me some gold coins telling me to go to your father. That she had sold herself for my sake I found out much later."

"What does that mean? You went to my father and told him a lie? This kind of lie is not only a crime, it is a sin."

"Yes, I have thought about it a great deal and still do. But not to treat a man like a man, to treat him worse than an animal without any cause, is the greater crime and the worst sin. I feel that in those five years whatever I learnt from your father is false, if not all of it certainly half. I don't know when it was, or how, or what kind of people they were who conspired, and managed through this kind of learning, to enslave others. At least half, no, more than half. And for generations!"

Jaidev felt that perhaps he had said too much about brahmins, his enemies. He said no more and Udambara saw both humility and helplessness in his expression.

"Perhaps you have now been able to understand," Jaidev pressed on. "This was the reason why I abandoned you on the banks of the Purusini and ran away. I couldn't bear the thought of spending a lifetime with you pretending to be a brahmin. Nor could I pull you down to a life of humiliation and poverty as a shudra. Both are terrible; they render a man inhuman, impotent – they strip him of dignity."

"Whatever you have said," Udambara responded after a while, "I have understood, in part though perhaps not entirely. But did you ever think about me? Now you tell me what I should do."

"Just think, Kalyani, that our marriage vows around the sacred fire were false, like a drama, but what is happening today is the reality."

"Simply by saying so you can't transform truth into untruth, nor the false into the real."

"To know the truth is a very serious matter. Without knowing the truth, it is not possible to begin to know it...."

Many days passed. Days turned into months.

Jaidev was promoted from being a scribe to being the public relations minister. He travelled with Raja Vishnu Varman, to Sakal (Sialkot), Sunetra (Ludhiana) and, most important of all, he showed great skill when negotiating with Chandragupta, the emperor of Magadha. But his counterpart in Patliputra, while discussing matters, had looked keenly at him and sniggered snidely saying: "It is hoped that 'Acharya' will keep his old associates in mind and also the interest of the emperor Chandragupta." He of course knew about Jaidev's shudra background.

Raja Vishnu Varman was thus often away from the palace. Sometimes he had matters of state to look into and sometimes he went hunting. When he was away Udambara would send Kanchanmala to call Jaidev on some pretext or the other.

That day too the Raja had gone hunting. Udambara sent Kanchanmala to call Jaidev saying that she had some important work with him.

Kanchanmala looked at Udambara thoughtfully and then went to tell Jaidev.

"What work can the queen have with me?" Jaidev asked Kanchanmala even though he understood perfectly why she had sent for him.

"How should I know? *You* should know, or the queen." She retorted with a hidden barb in her words.

"Right!" Jaidev said and started to get ready. Kanchanmala did not leave. She started tidying up. That is what she did whenever she came with a message or for any other work. In the beginning, when Jaidev did not have a servant, she would also go into the kitchen and cook for him.

Now, having folded and put away his clothes, she stood there looking at him.

"What is it? Do you have something to say, Kanchanmala?" Jaidev asked seeing her standing there and looking at him.

"No, nothing really," she responded shyly.

"But still…?"

"I was thinking…. I accused you and caused you to be flogged, yet you've never said anything to me."

"How was that your fault? You merely did whatever the Rani asked you to."

"So whose fault was it? I'm not really asking, just thinking aloud, and also thinking that you are not what you appear to be…."

"You are right there. What is apparent is not the truth. What you think is the truth. Sometimes even that is not the truth. Truth is limited by a person's ability to think."

"Are you talking about my limitations?"

"No, Kanchan. You too are not the same person as the way you are forced to act. If you had been born into a higher caste then perhaps...." Looking at Kanchanmala he fell silent.

At the palace, Rani Udambara enquired about Jaidev's wellbeing. Then for a long time she talked about this and that and asked how things were going in the kingdom. When it began to get dark Kanchanmala lit the lamp in the room and left. Jaidev tried to take his leave: "With your permission.... I really should go."

"If you want to go then why did you come?" Udambara asked looking at him soulfully.

"My mistake.... I think it would be proper for me to go, both for you and for me."

"Proper?" Hurt and anger flashed across Udambara's face. "Was it proper when you abandoned me by the river bank?"

"Don't shame me Kalyani by pointing out my shortcomings again and again. I understand your feelings."

"What do you understand? I am living as a wife with a man to whom I am not properly married, and with the man to whom I am married according to the ancient rites, with him I am forced to behave like a stranger!"

"It's not that I have never thought about this Kalyani. The truth of the matter is that I have little else to think of. Think of *my* suffering, Kalyani. I'm actually living in the garb of the enemy!

The fact is that we are both split personalities and neither of us has the courage to assume our true identity."

He remained silent for a while and then continued: "My father was born a defeated man, but at the end he tasted victory. I.... I, even after achieving so much, feel helpless, defeated."

Udambara watched his sad anguished face for a while and then said:

"I can only advise you to forget your past, that you were born to a boatman. The reality is that you are a learned pundit, a brahmin, a minister in this kingdom. Much more can happen in the future. Accept the present reality, don't grieve over what cannot be."

"I only want to be what I really am. But what is the reality? I still don't know whether I am a shudra or a brahmin, a pundit. Am I your husband or am I a traitor to the Raja?"

"Don't torture yourself unnecessarily. Man is nothing by himself. All his life man is carried along by the tide of time and by the waves of circumstance, changing every moment as he drifts along. You are not what you were that day on the banks of the Purusini, nor am I the same Kalyani who was eating figs on the udambar tree."

Udambara sighed deeply and, sitting close to Jaidev, her head on his shoulder, said: "Time is very powerful. We have to mould ourselves according to both time and circumstance...."

Raja Vishnu Varman had not gone hunting this time but was preparing for the 'hunt'. Jaidev's rise in the Raja's esteem and the status he had gained through his promotion had attracted the envy of the other ministers. When they found out about the increasing frequency of Jaidev's meetings with Rani Udambara they started to plant the seeds of suspicion in the Raja's ears insinuating that whenever he was away they took advantage of his absence.

It was for this reason that the Raja gave out that he was going hunting but he returned early. He ordered his soldiers to surround the Rani's palace and he himself went towards her chambers on tip toe, noiselessly. It was past midnight. The Raja had been informed by his spies that Jaidev had not left the palace. He was still inside with the Rani.

At precisely that moment Kanchanmala opened the door gently and said: "Excuse me Rani, the Raja is coming...."

Flustered, Udambara got up from the bed, straightened out her clothes, and looked at Jaidev, scared.

Jaidev too looked at her questioningly as though to say that there was no use in hiding anything now. There is only one way, that they tell him the facts without beating about the bush. Thus with one blow they would both be liberated....

They could now hear the footsteps of the Raja. Moments before the Raja could open the door Kanchanmala entered the room from another door; grabbing Udambara's arms she pushed her out of the room and stood next to Jaidev.

When the Raja stepped into the room, red in the face with anger and with his hand on the handle of his sword, he found Kanchanmala trying to cover her half naked body with her angavastra.

KANKI

Ramindra Ajit Singh

The cool light of the moon spread itself – on what?

On those beautiful plants which were remembering the exquisite hands which had planted them. They have grown so dense that one can see nothing underneath. But look! They are swaying to the rhythm of the gentle breeze. Perhaps they are humbly paying homage.

And the moonlight has lit up a tiny little cottage which can be seen clearly in the distance. Look! The path can also be seen now. It appears to be a very old path. There are many places where the stones are sunken. How many feet, how many legs; how many bodies must have weighed them down. Happily, the stones have no jagged edges, no broken bits. Perhaps they do not wish to cause a wayfarer pain. They cannot speak but they seem, all the same, to know about suffering.

Walking on that path, thinking the same thoughts,

Translated by Jasjit Mansingh

contemplating the suffering of all beings, I reach the cottage. I see an old door. It looks grimy, with grease marks on it but some parts of it are clean. The place seems peaceful, silent and quiet. I gathered up courage, lifted the bolt and banged it on the door. A muffled voice asked, "Who is it?"

I answered, "Please open the door, it is a traveller."

"Oh, no, brother! I have nothing and I live alone. What do you want from me? All I have are the clothes I wear, nothing, nothing else."

"Maiee, I've been travelling and I need a drink of water. I'm not a thief."

"Brother they all say that. Be on your way! You'll have to go the way you came, there is no way ahead."

"As you wish, I can't force you. If not here, I'll find shelter for the night under some tree."

The man got down from the step and started walking away.

The woman inside the hut got up and looked out of the latticed window. He was still close by. It was a long time since she had heard the voice of another human being. 'I have almost forgotten how to have a conversation. How shall I answer if he should ask me a question? Will I even be able to understand him?' she wondered. Then, with quick resolve, she opened the door and called out, "Brother traveller, have some water!"

The man heard and turned to look at me. He stood still for a moment and then returned. I fetched a jug of water and he drank deeply of it. I found myself saying, "O God-sent traveller, it is very late now. Eat whatever little I have to offer and you can rest here. When morning breaks drink some lassi and water and then go."

The man was silent. It seems he had heard nothing. Perhaps it was I who had heard nothing absorbed in my own thoughts. Or had I only spoken in my own mind? I tried again. "You have been sent by God. Spend the night here."

The traveller moved, lowered himself to sit cross-legged on the stone path and some time went by in silence. Then he spoke respectfully. "Mother, you are an old lady. If you don't mind may I ask you some questions?"

"Ask, but I don't know if I will be able to give you proper answers. It is years since I spoke to anyone. Here my only companions are the cow and the bull I have. I talk only to them. They understand me completely and I them."

In silence, at peace, the man thought, "You are a Devi," but he said, "May I ask your name?"

"Ask by all means but what good will it do you? Well, listen. It is Kanki."

"Kanki! What kind of a name is that?"

"Think of it as Kanki Devi. I am the daughter of the furrows of the field. My Father and Mother are Prithvi [the Earth] and Kanak [Wheat]...." I felt compelled to go on. "When the wheat was ripe in the field, in the fullness of its growth, awaiting a few more days of sunshine to be ready for harvesting, a very great saintly man came by. It was he who found me there. That good person told me how it had happened:

'The east wind was blowing hard, I saw the golden wheat in the fields rippling in the wind. As I marvelled at its beauty and thanked God for his bountiful creation I heard the cry of a baby. Desperate cries. Like a magnet they drew me … and I saw this lovely creature, with a beautiful face, dressed in elegant clothes, crying. I was taken aback, became fearful and upset. How did this little one reach here? Which heartless person could have abandoned her? Through my immense indignation a voice arose from within: 'This child is the daughter of the Earth. This is where she will be reared and you will be her guardian.' I reached down and picked up the child, and held it close to my heart. I saw also a small bundle lying there, and without thinking picked it up and brought it with me. In the hut I first gave the child some water and she fell asleep. Such an unbelievably beautiful face! Just seeing her gave me such satisfaction. I began to worry. I had never held a child before and now I would have to raise one! How would I manage? Suddenly I had a thought. I would seek the help of the woman who quietly brought food for me everyday. I waited for her. Yes, there was no other way….'

"That is how a faqir, a man who has given up all attachments to the world, found me, brought me up, educated me and taught me to pray to the Lord."

The moon had begun its journey to the western horizon. The traveller did not interrupt and Kanki continued speaking as much to herself as to him, remembering a time long past.

"Thus in innocence and playfulness I grew up under the shade of these trees, they were my playmates. I talked with them and I had the companionship of the blessed woman who brought simple food for me and for that man who was both father and mother to me. She used to come from a far away village... I grew tall and my body filled out. My clothes were always dirty. Sometimes my father would bring some almost new clothes and I would look at them and be happy. More time went by. One day while I was cleaning the cottage I moved a big stone which I had never been able to lift before. As I swept the broom over this it snagged on something. I looked and saw that it was a soiled bundle wrapped in cloth.

"I was afraid and drew my hand away from it. Then I thought I should see what it is that my father had kept there. He is a sadhu, he has renounced all worldly possessions. It couldn't be something that he was hiding from me. He is as clean as a mirror, and says that he has kept nothing hidden from me. Then what could this dirty bundle be...? Surely his Kanki can see it? Perhaps Father has just forgotten.... Kanki will take a look! She will then remind him...."

With trembling hands Kanki undid four knots and what did she see...?

"My hair stood on end. I lost all sense of reality, in fact I thought I must have lost my mind. I couldn't think straight. What was I seeing! It must be a dream.... Why on earth did I open it!

"In the bundle were four exquisite baby dresses! It seemed as though they had been newly stitched. And there was a little steel box, quite heavy. I opened it, and there lay, shining, some gold coins. A piece of paper too which had borne the passage of many seasons and become discoloured. There was something written on it but what did this unread daughter of Wheat and the Earth know of it. I put everything back as it was. I would ask what it was all about.... He is an old man, I thought, if I ask too many questions he may become upset...and what if he should leave me... what would I do? Who could I turn to? I was lost in such thoughts when I heard a knock on the door. My father had returned from the fields. He called:

'Kanki! Where are you? Come quickly! I have some guests with me.'

'Who is it, Father?'

'It is an old lady. Come, get her a drink of water.'

"I came out and saw her. My heart turned, it felt as though I had known her all my life. I greeted her with folded hands. I had thought of myself as old, but sitting next to her I saw she was even older. Father got up and went into the hut and the old lady asked me, "What do you think, Beti? Will you stay here or will you come to the orphanage?"

"I don't understand.... What is the orphanage?"

"What is your name, Beti? Tell me so I can use it."

"It is Kanki. Kanki."

There was a long pause. "Kan...ki. Kan...ki." She seemed lost in thought and then pulled herself together. "Right, Kanki it is....Child, I begin to understand." And she continued: "The orphanage – it is not far from here – is an old building. We all live there together, we sing devotional songs and we also work. Living together time passes pleasantly."

"But I'm fine here," Kanki responded without hesitation yet she wondered what was going on.

"I spend my time living the way my Father has shown me. Time passes beautifully, sweetly. I talk to my cow and bull, I wait for my Father to come home. He has taught me all I know. I don't even know how to talk to anyone else, so why should I go elsewhere?"

"Child, what has your father taught you?"

"When I was a toddler, running around and playing about, one day I came down with a strange delirium. It seemed as though the whole hut was shaking. When Babaji came home he saw that I was shivering and trembling. My face was flushed. My body was burning with fever. He fed me, spoon by spoon, something hot. He put his hand on my forehead and said, 'Recite, my child. Recite Wahe Guru, Wahe Guru. Keep reciting it, it will take away your suffering. It is the elixir of comfort and well-being. Your trembling will go.' Chanting Wahe Guru, Wahe Guru I dropped off to sleep. When my eyes opened I found that Wahe Guru Wahe Guru was still on my lips and I felt absolutely fine. Since that day, Deviji, I have never been parted from this wonderful medicine. This has been my constant companion. I cannot abandon this for anything else so please don't ask me to leave this place."

"It was Babaji, your father, who brought me here. He is concerned that he is very old now and worries about what will happen to you when he dies, you will be left alone in the world. In our place we all live together. If you come Babaji can also come and visit you there. Think of me as your father, as your mother. I will look after you, Kanki, my child. I will protect you from all suffering."

"But I said to the old lady that I would look after myself. I needed to think, I didn't understand exactly what she was saying...."

"The orphanage is a large, old building which belonged to a rich man who died young," the old lady continued thoughtfully. "He was heartbroken when he abandoned his infant daughter in the wheatfield, and could not bear the separation. The unfortunate mother of the child stayed on and spent her life looking for her child. At long last that unfortunate mother has found her abandoned child and the purpose of her life is fulfilled. The purpose of my life...."

Kanki stopped speaking. The moon had set and an early morning grey lightened the sky in the east. Day was about to break. The traveller picked himself up and said he would be on his way.

In the orphanage there was an air of excitement. The old lady's face glowed with happiness. She began to make preparations for Kanki's jubilant homecoming. Day ran into night and the sense of expectation rose higher.

A few days later she found her way again to the old cottage. She knocked on the door, and called out, "Kanki, my child, open the door! Your old mother has come." She knocked harder, and called out louder but there was no response. Disappointed she sat down on the stone path. A little later the old faqir arrived.

He opened the door, went inside and emerged carrying the old bundle of clothes. His hands were trembling, and his throat was choked with emotion. Eyes downcast, he could not speak. When at last he did, he said, "Old mother, our Kanki has gone. She is dead.... Here, take this.... Take it as a remembrance of Kanki!"

He broke down then, "Hai! Kanki is drowned in the river Ravi...Oh! Gone in the river..." He picked himself up and turned away from the cottage.

In stunned silence the old lady continued to sit. Out of her mind, she sat as still as the stones of the path.

MAA

Mohinder Singh Sarna

When she heard, it was as though a great shock wave had struck Bibi Rehmat in the chest. She was absolutely stunned. But, very quickly, with an immense effort of will she regained herself. It couldn't be! Ramzana was the biggest liar in the world! God knows from which gossip he had caught this rumour….

"Why did you go to Mughal Chak?" Bibi Rehmat asked her devar gently without either showing her distrust or accusing him.

"I went there to see a match for Nooran. It became late and I stayed over for the night. When I woke in the morning I found that the whole village had collected around Aalia."

So Ramzana was telling the truth. What he had said lodged in her heart like a blunt knife.

"Did you see it yourself?" The old woman asked in a faint voice, barely able to speak.

Translated by Jasjit Mansingh

"Of course. He was bleeding from one eye, and was lying there beaten to a pulp by lathis."

Bibi Rahmat felt herself go completely limp. She crumpled to the floor and lay in a heap. For a long time she could say nothing.

Finally she turned on him accusingly: "What kind of a chacha are you? How did you have the heart to leave the boy at death's door and come back here?"

"What chacha! Whose chacha?" Ramzana croaked even as his squint eyes flashed at her.

"Your son and his doings have brought disgrace to all of us here. And if Karim Baksh of Mugal Chak comes to know that Aalia is a relation of Nooran he will surely break off negotiations.... I ask you, couldn't Aalia have targeted any place other than Mugal Chak last night?"

Ramzana stopped for a moment as though waiting for Bibi Rehmat to say something and then continued: "People were saying that Mangal Shah had gone to Gujaranwala to file a police report. It was my duty to let you know. What you do next is your business."

When Ramzana, her husband's younger brother, had walked away Bibi Rehmat got a hold on herself and leapt to her feet. Helplessness would get her nowhere. If she continued to lie on the floor her precious son's blood, flowing from his eye, would course down the lanes of Mughal Chak.

From the tin of ghee she poured some into a smaller vessel, a lota. Into it she threw a fistful of almonds. She tied a few other things in the corner of her dupatta, slipped on her shoes and stepped out leaving the door ajar behind her. It was a distance of at least five koh, more than five miles, to the qazi of Mughal Chak. Walking along the sandy path her shoes filled with sand. She climbed on to the grassy path. When it seemed shorter, she cut across the fields on the bunds and foot paths or across patches of uncultivated land overgrown with vegetation. She was oblivious of the tall sarkanda grass slashing her face, her clothes torn and her body scratched by thorny bushes, or that her feet hurt on the coarse barren portions encrusted with gypsum. She pushed on with such energy that her age seemed to have no meaning. In her burning desire to reach her son quickly she hurtled on leaving all obstructions behind just as water flows overcoming all obstacles in its path.

The barbs her devar had unleashed rankled in her subconscious mind. Everyone knew of the misdeeds of her son! But there was a reason for his behaviour, something that was not generally known. After Alia got married, his wife Reshma didn't conceive. She wandered for seven years seeking the blessings of holy men and holy places. I don't know which mazaar it was where her vows bore fruit and at last she was blessed with a son. But it was as though it was too much for a withering branch to bear, or perhaps some other pir did not like what had happened. It was as though punishment was meted out. The fruit fell off the branch and was squashed under the feet of the pir.

Reshma went mad. One day she brought home a baby from the daughter-in-law of Khushal Chand Mahajan. He was an influential man and he had her committed in a lunatic asylum. That was the night that Alia first stole. He went to Khushal Chand Mahajan's house and took away all the things his wife had pawned to raise money for the delivery of her child.

From that day onwards Alia became a terror for all the mahajans, shahs, moneylenders and bakhtavars of the area. His wrath was particularly directed at the mahajans and moneylenders who treated the farmers no better than sheep to be shorn of the fruits of their labour twice each year.

She would simmer inwardly when she heard the stories about what her son had done. "Oh Son!" She would sometimes admonish him. "Why don't you show some sense? Your father did not behave like this, nor did your ancestors. Why are you ruining your life, adding rancidity where there should be only the tenderness of youth full of the flavour of the sweetness of milk?"

In the beginning she was unhappy but gradually she became accustomed to the situation. Moreover, she found that many people began to look towards her with gratitude in their eyes.

Alia, her son, just like the legendary Dhule Bhatti, used to loot the wealthy and the strong and distribute the wealth among the poor and disadvantaged. Like Dhule Bhatti he would help these poor people to get their daughters married and look after the expenses of the sick and the old destitute women who had no one to turn to. The moneylenders of the region hated him but the poor blessed him.

She ran. It was as though the fields and rough ground slipped away effortlessly behind her and Bibi Rehmat came closer and closer to Mughal Chak. Sometimes she would sigh deeply and in her heart there was the constant refrain: "Dear God, take my life if you will. But don't let my son come to harm."

Alia, lying there in Mangal Shah's courtyard, suffering the pain of his wounds did not turn to god, any god, for comfort. He had lost all faith in God's mercy, in fact even in his existence, ever since the day that his young, innocent and defenceless son had died having lived for only thirteen days. Now Alia could depend only on his own strength - his powerful arms and his legs like pillars built up through continuous exercise. Whoever, wittingly or unwittingly, had crossed swords with him had come to grief. When he had jumped from the roof of the haveli into the Shah's courtyard he had twisted his ankle and his head struck the dried stump of an old acacia tree. The impact of his fall shattered his left eyeball, he couldn't see through the blood and he fell. He regained consciousness when he was being beaten up by some people with heavy wooden sticks, the lathis they use for buffaloes. He could hear all kinds of voices.

"Careful! Don't let the bastard escape."

"Give the harami a good beating. Today we'll teach him how to be a man, this wretched offspring of wickedness...."

"Don't beat the son of a bitch to death! Leave him half dead, let the police come and they will finish the job.

Mangal Shah's servants had a field day. They rained blows on him and didn't care where they hit. They hit to their heart's content.

His hands burned with pain and the agony of his eye tortured him. His breathing was heavy and laboured like the sound of a ...mill.

It was the first time that he had been beaten so mercilessly. The physical agony he could tolerate but the humiliation he felt, the hurt to his spirit, rankled deeply.

Even though the lathi-weilding people stood all around him he attempted to get up. But the spasm of pain was too much and he collapsed again. He knew then that the game was up for him. He could do nothing to save himself and saying "Hai, Ma!" he resigned himself to his fate.

Just as he uttered, "Hai, Ma!" his mother arrived. The anger blazing from her bright shining eyes seemed to cast a spell on everyone. All those people who had been hurling insults moments before involuntarily lapsed into silence.

Even though Bibi Rehmat had the stoic endurance of a buffalo but when she saw what condition her son was in, she felt her throat choke, the blood drain from her face, her flesh sag and the heavy silver earrings in her ears hung loose. She was consumed by a desire for revenge. She wanted to attack his tormentors much as a swarm of stinging bees would, but she restrained herself.

She tugged at the string of a small black bag and emptied the bits and pieces it contained. Among them were a few pieces of charcoal, some sticks and bits of cane, a box of matches, seven red chillies with stalks, a bundle of alum and fifteen or twenty harmal-mustard seeds.

The young people in the courtyard thought that the old woman was getting ready for a performance. Others thought that she would do some black magic but the illiterate older ones knew that all these things were used to ward off the evil eye.

The old woman smoothed out the ground with the palms of her gnarled wrinkled hands. Then she lit the dried twigs and cane and put the charcoal on the kindling, blowing hard till the coals glowed red hot. She then placed the alum on the burning coals and passed the chillies and the harmal-mustard seeds seven times over her son's head before throwing them onto the fire. Then she took off her shoe and beat the lump of alum seven times.

Having done this she put her son's head on her shoulder and rocked it as though he was a little child and she held the lota with the ghee and almonds to his mouth.

"Have courage, my Son. Mother has come. Mother will help. May evil leave you. Come, you will be well. May the five pirs protect you. If Allah wishes you will ...."

She tenderly stroked each welt on his body, and with every caress of her hands it was as though he was infused with courage and strength. With every touch his pain decreased. Every limb of Aalia's body was becoming rejuvenated. The helplessness he had experienced vanished and in its place rose courage, a courage which surged through his body and vaulted through his veins.

Every caress of his mother was balm. The wounds inflicted by the rods on his back and chest became less prominent, and then they became faint, and as she continued they disappeared altogether. The colour of his skin, which had turned pale and anaemic, became again a healthy dark and his body began to shine like molten copper.

Suddenly he got up, bellowing a battle cry. Snatching a lathi from the person nearest him he brandished it threateningly. And before the headman of Mughal Chak knew what was happening Alia was well away – past the boundary of the village, beyond the reach of the law.

KAMAL

Manmohan Bawa

Whoever came in from Afghanistan to Hindustan to loot and plunder, whether it was Taimur Lang or Nadir Shah or Ahmed Shah Abdali, by the time he reached the banks of the Sutlej the invading force would have doubled or become three-fold. The Baluchis and Pathans who lived in the border states of Afghanistan and Punjab would join them lured by the prospect of easy riches. In the world there have been some countries, religions and people whose main profession has been loot and plunder.

In those days, near Dera Ismail Khan on the slopes of Mount Suleiman, there lived the Afridi clan of Pathans. When Ahmed Shah Abdali passed that way again with his army, two brothers, Naseeb Khan and Fateh Khan, set out with the forces. Naseeb Khan was in his late twenties and Fateh Khan was about forty. When he was leaving, Fateh Khan's Begum had tried to stop

---

Translated by Jasjit Mansingh

him saying: "Let it be. Enough is enough. It is not good to be too greedy." After the last raid, besides wealth they also had twenty horses and mares and more than two hundred sheep which grazed on the slopes of Mount Suleiman. They were quite well off. She also cautioned him that times had changed; no longer could they expect to go on horseback and return in a palanquin carried by slaves. "Now even the brahmins wear turbans and carry swords." But Fateh Khan had tasted blood. Besides wealth there were beautiful women to be had and the thought of such conquest was enough to spur him on, a new vitality raging through his blood.

The two brothers were returning with Abdali's army having looted and plundered all the way from Multan to Delhi. Bags full of gold and silver coins, bundles of fine clothes. Abdali reached the banks of the Beas river, pitched his camp and started building a boat bridge across the river. Occasionally a detachment would be sent out to collect food from one of the nearby villages.

While they were looting a house in Pakkhowal village Naseeb Khan happened to see the wife of the moneylender Kundan. It isn't that the women of his clan were not good looking but her exquisite beauty surpassed anything he had ever seen. His hand was in the bania's money chest but it did not move. On seeing Naseeb Khan, Kamal screamed and ran back into a room shutting the door behind her. The bania Kundan, when he saw the gold ornaments and silver coins being taken out of the chest, folded his hands and pleaded: "What are you doing, Khan Sahib? I am a family man. My children will starve... don't take everything." (That was a lie, he had no children.)

Naseeb Khan let everything fall back into the chest and said: "Right, I'll accept what you say, now you agree to what I say."

"What is that?"

"I'll return everything to the chest but then you give me your wife."

"No! No. How can that be? I... I..."

"What is this I...I...? Listen. If I want I can take both forcibly. It is because of my goodness that I am willing to strike a bargain with you."

"With my own money you want me to trade you my wife?"

The bania Kundan now regretted that when, a few months earlier, the young men of the village had joined the band of Sikhs, riding horseback and armed with swords, he had stayed back. Ever since Kamal had come to this house she had given him all her love, a mother's love, a sister's love and the love of a wife. She was one of those fortunate women who have a lot to give. Perhaps that was why he could not leave her and join the warriors. It was as though he had come to believe that nothing could go wrong as long as Kamal was with him.

Now he whimpered: "You'll have to kill me first. I will not allow you to take my wife as long as I live. If I can't fight, at least I can die."

"It is not difficult for me to cut off your head but the problem is that I have decided to marry your wife and I don't want her to think of me all her life as the murderer of her first husband."

Kundan picked up a heavy wooden stick that was leaning on the wall next to him and advanced towards Naseeb Khan in anger. Naseeb Khan reacted automatically throwing up his fighting arm and the spear he was holding pierced Kundan's shoulder. Kundan screamed and crumpled in a heap onto the floor. At that moment the door opened and Kamal, seeing Kundan lying there splattered with blood, went towards him. But Naseeb Khan intercepted her. Imprisoning her in his strong arms he collected his loot, threw her onto his horse like a sack and set off towards his camp.

Jassa Singh Ahluwalia, Hira Singh and Chhatar Singh and their soldiers were circling Abdali's camp like hungry lions. Abdali's army was superior in numbers and strength. That is why they remained at some distance from the camp. But if they got an opportunity they would launch a swift raid at night. And if they found a detachment patrolling they would pounce on it and quickly despatch it.

Sucha Singh, from Jassa Singh Ahluwalia's jatha, was patrolling that night with a detachment of fifty brave soldiers when he heard a woman's cries and the sound of horses' hooves. Sucha Singh signalled to his soldiers and they instantly drew their swords out of their scabbards and set off towards the sound of the hoof beats. When Naseeb Khan saw the approaching Sikh warriors on horseback he gave orders to his fifty Pathans to give battle and hold them while he himself raced away towards the camp. Sucha Singh left half his soldiers to fight and taking the rest gave chase to Naseeb Khan.

When Kamal saw the approaching Sikh warriors she flailed her arms shouting at the top of her voice, "Help! Help!"

"Don't worry, Bibi! I'm coming...," Sucha Singh called out as he lunged towards the Pathan swinging his sword at his neck.

But he was unsuccessful. In the nick of time Naseeb Khan managed to enter the safety of the camp. For Kamal this moment tormented her for many years and was her constant companion through all her miseries.

Abdali, just opposite the town of Goindwal, began to cross the river Beas on the boat bridge. When half his force, and his goods, had crossed Jassa Singh Ahluwalia's and Hira Singh's Sikh army attacked the rear. While Abdali tried to fend this off, on the other side of the Beas Lehna Singh and Gujar Singh blocked the way to Fatehabad. The battle raged on both sides of the Beas. The Sikhs looted whatever had not been taken across the river on this side and killed more than half the Afghans. But on the other side Abdali succeeded in saving himself. During the commotion of the battle the older brother, Fateh Khan, and Kamal escaped. They reached the other side but not the younger brother. Naseeb Khan's corpse lay on the sandy bank of the river, providing a feast for vultures and hyenas.

In the camp at the military stronghold of Fatehabad when Fateh Khan entered the tent he looked at Kamal. Kamal got up and remained standing. Her clothes were dirty, her hair uncombed and dishevelled, she had not bathed for many days. Looking at Fateh Khan's downcast face and ashen pallour she understood that something terrible had happened.

Fateh Khan spoke in anguish: "I don't know whether you'll be happy or sorry when you hear what I have to tell you. My dear brother who desired you so desperately is no longer in this world."

Hearing this Kamal felt as though someone had put balm on her wounds. She felt great peace in her mind. But in the very next moment she felt a kind of sorrow. It wasn't merely, "Now what will become of me?" For in the first few days, other than the eunuchs who guarded the tents, it was only Naseeb Khan who would sit next to her and talk with her. He would enquire about her well being. He even told her one day that he had returned to her village, secretly, putting at risk his life, to find out how her husband was. Kundan's wound was not serious and he had recovered. Now with Naseeb Khan dead, the repulsion she had felt gave way to a kind of sympathy. She raised her gaze once to look at Fateh Khan and then withdrew to a corner of the tent and lowered herself to the ground squatting on her haunches. Fateh Khan could not make out whether she was pleased or displeased at the news of Naseeb Khan's death.

As Fateh Khan came close to his home on the slopes of Mount Suleiman, he vowed to himself that he would never again set out on another such expedition.

In his tent he took out from his money belt the looted gold coins and the twenty silver rupees. Giving them to his wife, Rehana Khatun, he said: "Here, take charge of this. We looted much more but on the way the Sikhs took it all away."

"God be praised that you have returned home safe and sound. I told you before that the times have changed." Then she saw Kamal, dressed in dirty clothes, sitting in a corner behind him and asked imperiously: "And who is this? Haven't I forbidden you to ever bring home a woman?"

"I didn't bring her. It was your devar who abducted her."

"And where is he? He is not one to be shamefaced about anything."

"He has paid the price for the abduction. Where did these cursed Sikhs come from? The poor man was killed by them."

They were both silent for a while. Rehana Khatun was thinking about Naseeb Khan and Fateh Khan about Kamal. Then, pointing towards Kamal, he said: "She…she will be in your service. Think of her as your slave."

The next day, when Kamal had bathed and was properly dressed, she came before Rehana, Rehana saw how beautiful she was and she trembled inwardly. She sent for Fateh Khan and said: "I don't care what you do with her – throw her into the river Sindh or send her back home – I am not going to let her stay here with me."

"It is not so easy to take her back. There are bands of mounted Sikh soldiers every where, swords in hand. She, poor thing, cannot go by herself. And just think what price we have paid to bring her here."

"Don't make lame excuses. I understand what you have in mind. If she doesn't go I'll drive this dagger through her chest… or through mine."

Rehana Khatun was a formidable woman. Fateh Khan, brave as a hawk, could not stand up to her.

"Good Lord, what will become of me?" Kamal wondered as she stood there quietly. "My beauty itself has become my worst enemy!"

For centuries Multan city had been an important trading centre. It was also a centre for the trade in slaves. Earlier Hindu kings used to auction the women they had captured during their conquests at the crossroads of the town. Now the Muslim raiders sold Hindu women there. The religion and the faces of the looters changed, but the plight of women was exactly the same.

As they were going to Multan, Kamal pleaded with Fateh Khan that, however he could, he should leave her across the Beas. She would see to it that her husband paid him more than whatever he hoped to gain by selling her in Multan.

"Be quiet and keep walking!" Fateh Khan snapped at her. Actually he was not angry with Kamal but with Rehana Khatun. He continued: "You are talking like a fool! You know as well as I do that once a Hindu woman has lived in the home of a Mussalman her people will never take her back."

"Then...then why did you bring me here?" Kamal demanded firmly. "If this is the way you were going to treat me...? Just leave me here. Leave me to my own devices. I'll go wherever I have to go."

Fateh Khan was not prepared to do this either. He was greedy for the price she would fetch.

Three days later they reached Multan. He positioned her at the crossroads, half naked, and very soon, clutching a bag containing five hundred rupees, he turned towards home.

Four or five years passed.

The Sikhs had not won the whole state of Punjab but they controlled the area upto the river Chenab. Across the river there were constant skirmishes against Pathan settlements and their fortifications.

Jassa Singh Ahluwalia was fed up with the Baluchi Pathans of Mount Suleiman. He called up Lehna Singh's jatha and surrounded the area. Then dividing his forces into smaller bands he sent them in to teach the Pathans a lesson.

Sucha Singh encircled a village and ordered his Sikhs to set it on fire and reduce it to ashes. He also instructed them to bring whatever they could lay their hands on. He himself was a little tired from constantly fighting for twenty years. After fighting many big battles and over a hundred small ones he was amazed that he was still alive. Most of his companions had been martyred, one by one, in some skirmish or other. "Will this fighting, this destruction on both sides, will it ever come to an end?" he was thinking as he sat on horseback watching the flames leaping upwards.

"Excuse me, Singh Sahib," he heard a voice say hesitantly, and he looked up to see a soldier standing before him holding something in his hands.

"What's this?"

"Sir, it is a child. A boy about two years old," the young man replied.

"How do you know it is a boy?"

"His mother herself said so."

"The mother…? Do you mean his mother is still here? Didn't she run away along with the others?"

"No, Sir."

"Where is she?"

The Sikh soldier turned his head slightly to the right looking in that direction. Leaning against a tree a woman was standing there quietly.

"How did she get here?" But then he understood the situation himself. He dismounted and walked towards her.

"Were you left alone in the village or is someone else there?"

She didn't answer but continued to look down at the earth. The soldier standing next to her spoke.

"Some were killed, the others ran away."

"And her husband? I mean…." Sucha Singh asked.

The woman answered this question by shaking her head as though to say he was dead.

"Where do you come from originally?"

"P…p…Pakkhowal." The woman answered softly.

"Not that Pakkhowal which is close to Kapurthala? Across the Beas?"

"Yes."

"What is your name?"

"Kamal."

"Then could this be that same woman?" he wondered. The woman whom he had seen four or five years ago when he gave chase to a Pathan who was carrying her? Sucha Singh himself came from a nearby village.

"Don't you worry, Sister. You are quite safe now. Consider that you are with your brothers."

He put Kamal on a horse and set off towards Jassa Singh Ahluwalia's camp. It was a docile horse, moreover it knew Kamal very well because it had been captured from the same home where Kamal had lived for four or five years. Kamal couldn't believe that she was really free after all these years. Anyhow, right then she was neither sad nor happy. For, in a way, she had adapted to her life there and had even begun to feel at home.

When she had first got there, for two days she had remained withdrawn and just sat quietly in a corner. On the third day, her new master, Behram, had stood towering over her and roared at her:

"Get up! You slut! Sitting there as if you were royalty! Do you expect to be cajoled and fed….? I haven't bought you for nothing. I've paid five hundred silver rupees for you…!"

Kamal looked at him with dull, listless eyes.

"Get up and take charge of the kitchen without making a fuss. I have two small children. Can't you see? Their mother is dead and I have been left to bring them up!"

Behram had thought that he might even have to beat her up. But when she heard about the children she got up. What else could she have done?

From that day on Kamal gave him no reason to raise his voice, nor to be violent. Within a few days the children, one was four and the other six, became very fond of her. One was a girl and the other a boy. "Amma, Amma," they would call her and hug her and she began to enjoy that. Behram's old mother lived there too, stricken with pain in her knees. She too would come to her, stroke her head affectionately and say: "It is best for you, my girl, that you consider this to be your home. Horses and women have no independent existence. Whoever owns them calls the shots.... I too was brought here by his father from a Suleimani village."

"On the whole they were good days," Kamal was thinking about the past as she rode along towards Jassa Singh Ahluwalia's camp. They were good days because Kamal had no expectations of life. She made no demands. She endured. At first the Muslim women of the village used to taunt her, "Kafir, Kafir." Gradually they were won over by her personality and could not praise her enough. Now Kamal thought how she would miss her friends specially Sahiba Bano and Shabnam whom she would never see again. She, however, had the satisfaction of having her son with her.

After a while when Sucha Singh noticed that the child looked uncomfortable seated with Kamal on horseback, he drew close and lifted the child and held him in his arms.

Jassa Singh looked at Sucha's resolute face and saw that in his full beard a few white hairs glistened. Sucha had for many years been one of his bravest and most dependable companions. It was because of valiant Sikh warriors like him that the Sikh army had been victorious in many fierce battles.

"So then, brother, tell me what has been happening."

"Sir, this woman...."

"Yes, I see her."

" She says she wants to return to her home, Pakkhowal, across the Beas."

"Then do with her as we have been doing with the others. Reach her home."

"But she has her child with her, about two years old."

"And how long was she with the Pathans?"

"Sir, four or five years."

"So, that means that this child...?"

"Will she take the child to her husband's home?"

"Sir, she insists."

"This woman is a fool!" Jassa Singh said. "If she wanted to return to her husband then why did she bring the child? She should have left him there...let them look after their own!"

"But she says that he is *her* son."

"What an obstinate woman! Well. What is it to us? As is her will so shall be her fate." He thought a while and spoke again: "We are planning something here after a few days. We will be going forward. You take her and head for Kapurthala... your village is also somewhere there isn't it?"

"Yes, Sir."

"Until then send her to the langar so she can help there."

Kamal bathed. She discarded her Pathani clothes and put on the dress that Sikh women wear and she went to the langar. She was astonished to see the women there, all wearing kirpans, working like men. In another large tent she could see some women tending the wounded. In the langar she joined in to make the rotis. At night, after the kirtan, there was ardas : "The Khalsa will rule, none will go hungry." Seeing the enthusiasm of both men and women and their aspirations she felt that she had entered a new world, a world full of hope. While living in the Pathan village she had felt the whole of Punjab would be under the heels of the Muslims but here she was witnessing quite a contrary reality.

Labh Singh, of Sucha Singh's jatha, had been wanting to go home on leave for a long time. His village too was in the same direction. Both of them and Kamal set off on horseback towards Kamal's village. Labh Singh sat the child between his legs on his horse. After a while the child started crying and Labh Singh was not able to quieten him. Finally he said, "It seems he wants to pee."

"He doesn't want to pee. He is just uncomfortable. Pass him to me." Riding along Sucha Singh took the child from him and held him in the crook of his left arm in such a way that the child was neither jolted nor uncomfortable. Kamal glanced quickly sideways at him in gratitude and rode on.

By the time night fell they had reached a large town. Kamal broke her silence and asked: "What town is this?"

"Multan. Have you been here before? It is a large town."

"Oh!" Kamal felt a strange stirring within. It was here, at the crossroad, half naked, that she had been sold.

Making enquiries, they reached a sarai. The sarai keeper opened one room for them.

"Hey! Don't you see that my sister is with me? Give her a separate room."

Just before this Kamal had been speculating where they would spend the night, and how, with these two strangers. When she heard Sucha Singh use the word 'sister' it was as though a great peace descended in her heart. It seemed that she had met a humane being for the first time.

They travelled for four or five days, staying in gurudwaras and dharamsalas, until at last they came to Goindwal on the bank of the river Ravi. As usual Labh Singh and Kamal dismounted first. Then Kamal reached up to take her son from Sucha Singh. After arranging for rooms, Sucha Singh settled Kamal in and he himself went out to a halwai to get milk for the child. Giving it to her he said:

"Here. Let him drink this. Then we will go to the langar and eat."

The next morning, before they took the boat, Labh Singh took Sucha Singh aside and said:

"All is well. After you have crossed the river you will reach her village after noon."

"And you?"

"If you permit me I'll carry on to my village now. It is very close from here, next to Khadhur Sahib. Otherwise I'll have to cross the river again, alone. It will take another two days."

"Okay. Go."

"Thanks. But when you go back don't tell Jassa Sardar."

The flat bottomed boat was quite large. It accommodated the horses, goats, and about fifteen or twenty people. The boat set off, cleaving through the waves. The dark bodies of the boatmen glistened in the sun, the oars swished and there was complete silence. Then the child said something, in Pashto.

The passenger next to him, who seemed to be a brahmin, screwed up his nose and moved away a little. And then said to the person next to him:

"Just look! The child speaks Pashto! Is the woman a Hindu or a Mussalman?"

"Think for yourself, Pundit. Such women....! He must be the offspring of some Muslim."

Hearing this Kamal was close to crying, her eyes filled with tears.

Sucha Singh glared at both of them and said: "Can you both swim?"

"Why?" The man next to the brahmin plucked up enough courage to ask.

"If you don't know how to swim then why are you blathering?"

Both of them looked at Sucha Singh who was actually prepared to pick them both up and throw them into the river.

In the bazaar at Goindwal someone had made similar remarks and Sucha Singh had pushed him hard against the wall.

" Don't for my sake pick a fight... these people are not worth fighting with."

"You don't worry, Bibi. It is not for nothing that I have survived for twenty years – fighting off such cutthroats."

Having crossed the river, they mounted their horses again and continued. Seeing that Kamal looked a bit worried Sucha Singh said:

"Don't be upset. We'll reach your village in two or three hours."

"He doesn't even know," Kamal said.

"So what?"

"I will be judged by this child."

"You were saying that he loved you very much? I mean...."

"Yes.... But that was a long time ago."

"Hunh!" Thinking about this Sucha Singh also began to worry.

As they rode through the village, the sound of hoof beats caused a peculiar reaction. The men were out in the fields working. The women watched from their doorsteps or from their windows. Kamal was wearing Punjabi clothes and she had half covered her face with her dupatta.

Seeing two people dismount in front of his house Kundan Lal looked at them with curiosity.

"Lala, have you recognised who this is?" Sucha Singh asked as he came closer. As Sucha Singh pointed to Kamal, she pulled the dupatta away from her face and Kundan Lal's face lit up with joy.

"Kamal! Are you really Kamal?"

The same rounded face. The eyes seeking approval, full of hope. The problems she had faced and the experiences endured gave her face a strange poignancy. Then Kundan saw the child Sucha Singh was carrying. An unknown fear gripped him and he shook as he asked:

"Who is this?"

"This is Kamal's son."

"Kamal's or some Mussalman's?"

"Don't get upset for nothing," Sucha Singh said firmly. Jassa Singh's orders were that when such women who were abducted by the Pathans have been rescued from them they should be taken to their own homes. And if someone declined they should be forced into accepting them. "Just think about her, how much she must have suffered in these four or five years. How can this poor woman be blamed for this? The fault is ours for not having been able to provide her sufficient protection. But have no fears now, now the rule of the Khalsa has been established throughout Punjab, the rule of true Punjabis even if it is after seven or eight hundred years.

"That is all very well, but I cannot keep this child."

"Have you no...."

"I can tell you that no one else would have agreed to accept a woman who had spent five years in the home of another man."

"Ram accepted Sita."

"Then he threw her out again."

"But a lot happened in the interval between the two events. At this moment it is best that we put these things out of our minds."

"I'll try to forget, but only if she will get rid of the child who is someone else's and come to stay...."

"This...this is *my* child!" Kamal cried out as though something deep within her had erupted. For too many days, for too long, had she passively allowed others to toy with her life. Now she felt as though everything was unreal and she continued in a cold and measured way:

"Listen, Lalaji. The man who took me away from here sold me. The man who bought me did so by spending his hard earned money – five hundred rupees of it. Because he paid he had a right to me."

"You...! Aren't you ashamed to be talking this way?" Kundan spluttered.

"Shame? It is people like you who ought to be ashamed, people who consider a woman to be a commodity to be bought and sold or an object to be enjoyed."

Kundan had never known Kamal to speak like this. He spoke in some surprise, "What are you trying to say?"

"Can't you understand such a small and simple thing? I have been silent for too long but today I shall have my say. The man...man has no relationship with a child. His only connection with the child is simply a momentary union. The woman nourishes the child in her womb for nine months giving her blood, her all...." She continued talking in this vein for sometime and then, taking her child from the arms of Sucha Singh, she held him close to her chest. Hugging him tightly she said:

"If you cannot keep my child then there is no question of my staying with you."

Kundan, stupefied, speechless, stood there gaping at her.

"Come, Singh ji," Kamal said. "He just cannot understand what I am trying to tell him." She turned and started walking away quickly as though she could stay there no longer.

Out of the village they mounted their horses once again and rode on in silence. After a while they reached a place where the path bifurcated. Sucha Singh reined in his horse and said:

"Now, Bibi, what will you do?"

Kamal looked at him questioningly.

"I am asking because one of these paths goes to my village. I'll be staying there for four or five days before I return."

Seeing the concern in Sucha Singh's face, Kamal said: "You must be thinking that I want to go and drown myself in the river. Well, if I didn't die after what I went through for five years, there is no point in dying now."

"Then...?"

"To reach where I am thinking of going, I need one or two trustworthy guards. I have some money hidden away. I can pay them a daily wage."

"Guards?"

"Yes. Because I am alone, a woman, and moreover there is the child."

"But where...?"

"From where I have come."

"Where do you mean?"

"I want to bring up my son to be such a man from whom no one would dare to or be able to abduct a woman.... I wish to...."

"I understand." Sucha Singh knew what it was that she wanted and he was pleased. "Then, Bibi, come with me to my village and we will go on together after three or four days."

Drawing his horse alongside hers, he said: "Come. Pass the boy to me...."

SARDARNI

Buta Singh

The haveli was in the centre of the village, close to the big well in the chowk from where all the village folk fetched water. By the side of the well stood the majestic banyan tree – once known as 'Bahmanan da pippal' – the pipal of the brahmins. This banyan of the well was once the glory of the haveli. There was a time when the haveli was known as the Haveli of the Zaildars. Gradually it became the Haveli of the Nambardars. But now both these names have faded away and people simply refer to it as the Shahs' haveli.

Names have significance because of men whose footprints leave a mark on the very earth itself. With those zaildars and nambardars gone, the names too followed them into oblivion. The structure of the haveli and its name, just like the unused well, developed a thick layer of mud, a crust of mud.

The Shahs' haveli!

Translated by Tara Meenakshi Sekhri

Whenever there have been Shahs everything has been ripped apart just like a split watermelon. And what is left is a hollow shahdom of three wings of the haveli. Even a beggar is not sure of receiving alms from any of the inhabitants of the three homes. Mighty Shahs indeed!

The elders knew that at one time the haveli was considered to be the patron of the entire village. But now only three brothers are left. And they too are separated. They live around a common courtyard, unhappily. The land has been divided, and the cattle. Even the beds and linen. Soon brick walls will come up between them. The only thing that is left to each one of them is possession of the three wings of the haveli. So much for the Shahs' haveli!

The wives of the younger brothers Achhar Singh and Sadhu Singh tried their utmost to bring about a complete separation. But what of it? When the land, and things – even pots and pans - have been divided then what does it matter if the kothis too are apportioned. It would put a stop to these daily quarrels once and for all. When there is no communication at all, then why be saddled with the burden of a common wall?

Each brother's sons are now growing to be young men. What if the two younger brothers come to blows even as they tie the bull to the common peg in the courtyard? God forbid that tensions flare up and they slaughter each other over trivialities. What can they have in common when there is no interaction, no communication between them?

The two younger sisters-in-law were intimate with each other, sharing confidences, conspiring. But neither they nor their husbands, Achhar Singh and Sadhu Singh, had the courage to stand up to their elder bhabi, Tej Kaur, the eldest daughter-in-law of the family.

Tej Kaur was tall and imposing, robust, and had a wheatish complexion. When charged with emotion, she would stand erect with her hands on her ample waist and hips. When she spoke she would be so firm and precise that many a lion's heart would tremble. No one could think of an appropriate reply. She was the eldest. Both her husband's younger brothers, and their wives, called her Bhabi and gradually the whole village came to address her as Bhabi. People would bring their disputes to her. Not only the workers, even mothers-in-law and daughters-in-law came to her with their problems, and she settled their disputes with fairness. They would come crying and go back happy.

The two younger brothers held her in awe and could never dare to stand up against her, their bhabi who was like a mother. It was she who planned our weddings and brought our dolas home, welcoming our wives. She fulfilled all the rituals for our well-being, made the sacred offerings to the gods to avert the influence of the evil eye, blessing us, and sprinkling the purifying water to welcome our brides when they stepped into this house. How can we now disregard even her slightest wish? Now everything has been divided. All that is left is the haveli.

Tej Kaur and her sisters-in-law do not speak to each other any more. When a child asked for something, he would get a tight slap on the face and be admonished: "We do not want anything from your Taiji's place. We have nothing to do with her, not in life, nor in death!" The tirade would then be deflected but continued: "Our husbands are spineless, like limp ragged quilts! They are as scared of her as crows are of a catapult! God alone knows when the matter of these bricks walls will be settled...."

Months would go by without the brothers talking to each other even though they shared the same haveli.

Tej Kaur was adamant. She was firm about one thing despite all the other divisions – lands or cattle. "The haveli cannot be divided while I am alive – the Haveli of the Zaildars, of the Nambardars. The Shahs' haveli will not be reduced to the level of separate kothas of Gopal Singh, Achhar Singh and Sadhu Singh! This cannot happen. The haveli is like a fortress. There are two ber trees, one shahtoot tree, one banyan tree – place the charpais where you please, tie the cattle where you wish. When I die you can think about dividing the haveli.... Build a dividing wall in the middle of the courtyard? Never! You'll have to cut my throat first. If you are the sons of Sandhus, know that I too am the daughter of a Gill sardar, one who didn't hesitate to chop off a head or two even if it should be that of his own sister's son or his brother's son!"

Tej Kaur remembered the time when she was a small girl and there was a terrible fight among her cousins, her father's brother's sons. Everyone brandished sticks, striking out, hitting hard. So much so that several men from both families were so badly hurt that they had to be taken to the civil hospital. There they lay, members of both families, with broken bones. Her middle brother Sarjit had fractured an arm and a leg while many others had broken ribs. Bebe, her mother had not been unduly perturbed. She had thanked God that it was only broken arms and legs, and that their lives, on both sides of the family, had been spared. Oh God! What if anyone's throat had been cut? It would have been more than she could have taken.

Bebe immediately got pitchers full of milk and large tins of ghee loaded on Radu Mehra's back sling and went to the hospital. The wounded lay facing each other, one row for each family. Bebe mixed ghee into hot milk and gave it first to her elder uncle's sons saying: "Get up, my lions! Drink this milk and ghee and get strong. The matter is not over yet. The problem will not end until three or four women are widowed in the process…." Bebe kept feeding milk to her elder uncle's sons, Shivdev Singh and Harbans Singh. She would hug them and urge them, with a lump in her throat: "Shivveya! You simpleton! Tell your mother to feed you ghee and milk. See? With just a few blows you have landed in hospital….! Bebe kept pressing Shivdev to her breast, and as she talked to them she had tears in her eyes. The cousins, her taya's and chacha's sons, lying on beds facing each other, listened to her quietly. None had either the courage to retort, or even the heart to reply.

"I am the daughter of the same mother, O! Achhar Singh and Sadhu Singh! You two are henpecked husbands! Try and dismantle the haveli, but remember with each falling brick you will be breaking my limbs!"

Who could face the wrath of this lioness? They were marking time. Everyone went about his own business and the days went by in the same haze of swollen faces and attitudes.

Sadhu Singh was the youngest. He was inordinately proud of the fact that he had three sons, all studying in the higher classes, and no daughter to worry about. The father of sons is no less than a king. 'What do I want from this dilapidated moth-eaten haveli? Let her keep it to herself – the profits and the losses. She thinks she is some kind of royalty, a princess! Well. She can keep on thinking so for all I care!'

Sadhu Singh's ardent desire was to own another pair of handsome bullocks, and his greatest love was for the pair he kept. He often said: "Capable sons and pairs of fine bullocks are the pride and ornament of a jat's haveli. As for land, everyone has it. Some have less, some have more."

He had a unique pair of Nagauri bullocks with tall humps, long horns, and shining white bodies. During the wedding season Sadhu Singh was much sought after. If the newly wedded bride was to be taken in a decorated bullock cart, then his Nagauri bullocks were harnessed to drive the cart, their backs adorned with a richly embroidered cover, a frill around the edges. They looked so magnificent that people would forget to look at the bride as they gloated over the bullocks.

He often dreamt of getting another pair so that he wouldn't have to refuse anyone. Moreover there would then be more excitement at home.

Sadhu Singh spent many months in search of a good pair. One evening he brought home a precious calf of Sahiwal breed. He was about a year old, perhaps a little more. Such resplendent skin! Snow white hooves. A beauteous patch on its forehead.

Well formed flanks and a stout body. The very sight of the calf made his heart dance in joy. He loved to watch it, tied to a peg in the haveli. He brought a big cake of jaggery. Breaking it into pieces, he would feed it to his pet, one piece at a time. Rubbing its back lovingly he would say: "Bless the cow that gave birth to you!"

Tej Kaur watched from her door stoop as Sadhu fed the calf. Her heart went out to him. He was her devar, but she felt he was like her own younger brother. She had virtually brought him up as her son. Fights and quarrels are all part of family life. She wanted to go and congratulate him, but her feet wouldn't move. She consoled herself – 'Sadhu Singh is a fool! What good will a single calf do? Sheer indulgence in an entirely unnecessary expenditure!'

Then Tej Kaur's elder son's brother-in-law came to visit. He stood behind her and said: "Maasi, why are you standing there so tight-lipped?"

"Oh Shingara, you! Sadhu Singh has brought a bull calf. It has brought cheer and excitement to the inner courtyard. Once it is full grown, how grand it will look!" Tej Kaur said and she went inside.

Shingara sat recalling what his sister had warned him about. "Dear brother! Don't visit or meet my aunts. My mother is very angry and cross with them. If she sees you talking to them she'll get after you!" But here was Bebe, full of joy and pride in the calf bought by her devar. It was as though it was tied in her own back yard.

Shingara liked the calf immensely – rust-brown in colour with a darker shade along its neck. And the beauty mark on its forehead! The four hooves were so white! He approached Sadhu Singh who was sitting on the charpai near the ber tree and greeted him respectfully.

Sadhu acknowledged his presence warmly and shot a barrage of questions. "Come! Welcome, O Virk sardar! How are you? Fine? How's life? How are you doing? When did you come?"

"I came the day before yesterday, Maasad ji. The whole village is so proud. Everyone is talking about your calf! It is indeed a feather in your cap. Maasi says this courtyard has come alive with joy and excitement. " Singara replied as he stroked the calf on its back and hump. The animal felt the loving caress and a tremor ran through its entire body. Now Shingara addressed the calf. "Oho! Why are you so shy? I am part of this family my lovely one!" And he continued to rub the flanks, pat its forehead and, running his hand down the length of its body, held its tail firmly and gave it a loving tug. It seemed that the calf felt comfortable that this person was not a stranger.

Sadhu Singh reared this calf very diligently. He would walk around it at least five or six times a day. He would sit next to it talking of this and that. Shingara too would join him and rub its neck and back and pet it. He would even let it lick the palms of his hands. And he looked at it in a slightly strange manner.

It so happened, almost as though God willed it, that night there was a mild drizzle causing a bit of commotion in the courtyard. Since there was a little nip in the air Sadhu Singh shifted his bed indoors, made himself cosy and fell fast asleep.

At day break, when he awoke, the calf was missing.

Sadhu was stunned. He was at his wit's end. He tried to reassure himself that it must have broken loose and wandered out of the gate. But he himself had closed the big gate of the haveli before going to bed! Yet he went outside and ran about looking everywhere. There was not a sign of the calf. As the day advanced he got really worried. The disturbing news of the calf having been stolen spread throughout the haveli. The villagers too remarked: "Not so much as a needle has ever been stolen from the haveli, how could such a theft have been committed at the Shahs'. Theives have walked away with their cattle!"

When Bhabi Tej Kaur learnt of this she came out promptly and saw Sadhu Singh lying flat on his face on the charpai. She leaned over him and shook his shoulder asking solicitously, "Sadheya, what's wrong?"

"Bhabi, the calf has been stolen!" He answered, turning to look at her.

"Oh you great Sandhu! Where the hell were you? Were you dead or alive? You were sleeping close by and thieves unfastened the calf and took it away?" She roared at him standing in the centre of the haveli. Gopal Singh heard her thundering voice and came out. So did her other brother-in-law and his sons. She turned on them and berated them all at an even louder pitch.

"Are you a family of petty weavers? What happened to your Sandhu valour? Had you chopped off the head of the thief who had come to steal your calf I would have acknowledged you to be the true sons of the Sandhu sardars, real Zaildars."

When Puro, her daughter-in-law, Sadhu's wife, heard Bebe Tej Kaur roaring in the courtyard she trembled from head to foot. The words echoed in her ears – "Had you chopped off the head of the thief who had come to steal your calf I would have acknowledged you to be the true sons of the Sandhu sardars, real Zaildars!"

Puro collected herself and calmed down. She began patting her little daughter, one-and-a-half-years old, whom she was holding in her lap. But still she could not shut out Bebe's remarks. The words rang in her ears and pierced her heart.

Then Tej Kaur confronted her husband and said sharply: "Why are you all gaping at me as though at a monkey show? Take Sadhu and go to the police station!"

So, the three brothers and Tej Kaur's eldest son, Dalip Singh, reached the thana. The Thanedar knew, of course, that this was the most affluent family in the village but he was a bit puzzled to see all the brothers there together. Guessing the Thanedar's thoughts, Gopal Singh bellowed an explanation at him. "Chaudhri ji, it is not just a matter of losing a calf. Our prestige is at stake! Ours is such a big haveli – it has about twenty-odd people living in it – and someone just untied the rope and stole the calf? Once we know who did it, we will kill him! Right now! Today we have been proved to be no better than idiots...."

The Thanedar replied curtly yet sympathetically. "Gopal Singh! This is a police thana not a bania's shop! You have come to us, and we will take legal action. We will conduct a proper investigation. How dare a theft take place in our vicinity!"

The report was written. The brothers and nephew returned home looking gloomy as though they were returning from a funeral. On the fourth day they went to the thana again to enquire.

"Chaudhri ji, have you found any clues so far?"

"Gopal Singh, the calf is in your own house." He smiled and added: "Had the calf not been within the family, we would have dragged the thief here and dealt with him. Just because of you we have thrashed many scoundrels in the village, unnecessarily!"

"The calf.... In our house?"

"Yes."

"Don't talk in riddles, Chaudhri ji! Just tell us the truth." Gopal Singh demanded trying not to show his impatience.

"Your calf is in the house of your kudum. Your daughter-in-law's brother has walked away with it. Since you are all related by marriage you'll surely become good friends again soon. But I swear by God, if he were not Dalip Singh's brother-in-law I would have beaten up that Shingara with shoes and flayed him! He would then have known the true worth of a Virk sardar!"

Upon hearing these loud harsh words of the Thanedar, Gopal Singh and Sadhu Singh hung their heads in shame and embarrassment. Dejected, with hands clasped behind their backs, they slunk back home. Tej Kaur was waiting at the threshold of the haveli. Impatiently she darted her question.

"Have they found a clue?"

"Hmmm! They have…. The culprit is right here! Under our noses!"

"Don't needle me! Talk straight, and clearly O Sardar." She demanded in a firm, strong voice.

"My dear wife," her husband began. And continued: "I can hardly speak…. Cut my nose, and with my own knife? It is Dalipa's brother-in-law Shingara who has stolen our calf!"

"Shingara! Shingara?" Tej Kaur asked incredulously as she wrung her hands.

""Yes, yes! Am I speaking Pushto? Can't you understand!" Gulab Singh shot back, full of rage.

No sooner did Tej Kaur hear this, she took command. "Eh, Sadheya!" she roared at Sadhu Singh. "Saddle the mare! Go right now to Ghummani. If you are a man, return with the calf. Don't let that thief escape, or else I'll sort you out! Come back by evening. No harm will come to the horse – the distance is only ten kos."

When Sadhu Singh heard his Bhabi's clear and strict instructions, and that thundering voice, he ate two or three chapatis hurriedly, washed them down with a bowl of lassi, and started for Ghummani.

As he rode he kept thinking, 'Oh Shingara! Damn you. Couldn't you find any other house to steal from? Good Lord! Did you have to burgle your own sister's house? Now it isn't a matter of a few hundred rupees…. Bhabi will not spare me… she'll be after my life!"

He was still thinking such thoughts when he reached the

home of the Virk sardars and stopped the mare in front of the main sitting room. Shingara's father, Chet Singh, and his uncle, Ujagar Singh, were there. Chet Singh alerted Ujagar Singh with a conspiratorial look as though to say, "Here comes the owner of the calf!" Ujagar smiled and whispered, "Brother, don't worry. Let the knave enter." He then stood up to welcome Sadhu Singh. He spread a checked rug on the charpai and placed a cushion, the cover adorned with a floral design, on it. He called out loudly to his sister-in-law. "Bring a bowl of milk and also something to eat. Sardar Sadhu Singh is here."

They then started a conversation about this or that. The two brothers did not give Sadhu Singh a chance to speak. "Brother, you haven't eaten anything at all. Won't you try some of these sweets…" and so on. But Sadhu Singh could only visualise his Bhabi Tej Kaur standing, her hands on her hips, and hear her thunderous voice, "You are a Sandhu sardar, and the boy's uncle too! Talk loud and clear. Be firm!"

He plucked up some courage and spoke.

"Bhaiyya ji, it is a very unpleasant matter. Even the mention of it is embarrassing…. Shingara is still a child, but he has done something wrong. He untied our calf and has brought it home. He must now be quite satisfied with the thrill of keeping it so kindly restore the calf to me. I should get back to my village before sunset. My folks will be waiting for me…."

"How much did you pay for the calf, Sadhu?" Uncle Ujagar asked, and continued making light of it. "It must have cost about eighty rupees, perhaps ninety? Here, you take a hundred and twenty-five and let's call it quits. The lad took a fancy to it and brought it home. Tell me, brother, how can we break the boy's heart? Isn't Shingara your son as much as he is ours?"

When he heard such composed and loving words Sadhu was tempted to accept the money offered and go back. He felt that it would do no good to argue and complain to his relatives by marriage about one of their own. But then he saw in his mind's eye Bhabi Tej Kaur and imagined the tongue-lashing he would get: "Eh! Are you Sandhus or weavers? You took the hundred and twenty-five rupees? Stick the money on your forehead! On your brother's forehead too! Oh why was I married into this family of weavers!" Sadhu Singh shuddered at the thought of it and tried to take a stand.

"Bhaiyya ji, with your blessings there is no dearth of money in our family. We only want our calf back." But it didn't work. Chet Singh and his wife Bal Kaur also pressed Sadhu Singh to accept the amount that had been offered but nothing came of it.

Sadhu Singh returned to his village empty-handed, hanging his head in shame.

Even before he arrived, Tej Kaur had dropped in several times. Her heart was on fire. She had been itching to harness a horse and set out to her kudums' herself. But then she argued that men's work was best left to men. Tej Kaur was sitting on the charpai in the middle of the courtyard looking expectantly towards the gate. She even felt her neck stiffening.

When Sadhu Singh reached and related the entire episode, Tej Kaur screamed in frustration. "First they steal, and now they are trying to be smart and clever! These are our kudums! Shameless people! Don't they realise whom they are dealing with? Scum! They've become too high and mighty. Remember the story of the acrobat woman who was doing her act, walking and dancing, on a rope at a height? Well, she saw her in-laws and quickly climbed down from the rope. She had such respect for her sambandhis. And here these 'respectable' sardars showed no consideration for their daughter's uncle-in-law who had come from such a distance – ten kos! Like the elder brother, so the younger. They had better remember that they have given their daughter in marriage to this haveli, the Haveli of the Zaildars!"

Puro was petrified when she heard Bebe's powerful voice reverberate through the haveli. She felt like jumping into the well in front of the haveli and putting an end to her life. "Oh Shingara, God help you! You have strewn thorns in a happy, settled family."

Once again Bebe's commanding voice rang out. "At dawn Dalipa and I will proceed to Ghummani. How dare they not return our calf?"

Early the next morning mother and son prepared the horses and set off. Before noon they dismounted in front of the haveli of their kudams. As soon as she saw Tej Kaur, Shingara's mother's heart froze. When she noticed Dalip Singh with her, she heaved a sigh of relief. Though she was like a mad tigress at the moment surely she would mellow down and become considerate in the presence of her son. With this thought in mind, Shingara's mother ran out to greet and embrace her kudumbani and she touched her feet respectfully. There was much hustle and bustle in the house. Cots were placed in the courtyard. But no matter how brave and bold one is, when the enemy arrives unexpectedly, one is bound to be nervous. Before Shingara's mother had time to observe the proper protocol and enquire after the well-being of their family, Tej Kaur took the bull by the horns, so to speak, and spoke in a stern voice.

"Look, Bibi! This is our second trip to your place. This kudamadhari, this relationship of ours through the marriage of our children, is like the fragrance of flowers. This sweet smell can disappear and give place to an ugly stink. Return our calf to us. It will be good for both our families."

"Bibi, why do you talk like this?" Bal Kaur replied trying to deflect the anger. "We are not running away with your calf, are we? Nor is the calf going anywhere. We may be two different households but it is the same family.... First have a glass of water and relax. We'll talk about all this in a while."

Tej Kaur mellowed a little but was not one to be sidetracked. "Oh Sardarni. The matter has to end with discussing the calf, so why don't we just start with that and finish it?"

"Bibi, don't talk like this.... I told Sadhu Singh that once the bones are immersed in water they are gone forever. No one can retrieve the bones from running water. Please take twice the amount of money from us – we are neither denying nor refusing anything! It isn't really our fault, the boy is an ignorant fool! He has made this mistake. Please forgive him, and accept this money for the calf. We respect you as our superior."

"Bhaiyya ji, if *you* need money, a thousand rupees or two

thousand, we'll give it to you. Money is not the point. I have not come to retrieve bones from the Ganga. I have come for my calf. God forbid that we might have to shut the mouth that has swallowed our bones. Don't you know that I am the daughter of Gill sardars? Relations by marriage be dammed. The calf is ours. We want it back."

"Bhaiya ji, you probably estimated that Sandhus are disunited. That they can be won over, one by one! You are wrong. Restore the calf, or we shall do our worst...." Dalip Singh put in angrily and he raised his arm which inadvertently struck the bowl of milk which his mother-in-law was carrying for her guests. The bowl fell and the milk spilled onto the ground.

Now spilling milk, specially in their own home where a kirpan hung on every peg in the wall, was an ultimate insult for Virk sardars. Sardar Chet Singh stared hard at his son-in-law, as though he wanted to break this cur's neck and throw his head away. He vented his anger silently in his mind: "What! Do we have no dignity or respect? Look how he jerked the milk bowl and spilled the milk in the courtyard! It doesn't matter if one daughter of our family becomes a widow, we will kill four men and make four widows in their family!" Before he could utter a word, Tej Kaur quickly cleaned and dried her kudamani's arm using her own fine silk shawl and reassuring her: "Don't be angry, Sardarni! It was a mistake, he didn't mean to knock the bowl down."

"It doesn't matter, Bibi. To me Shingara or Dalip Singh are alike. But why are *you* cleaning the floor?" Shingara's mother exclaimed and pulled her away by the arm as she called out, "Oh Rukko! Come here! Clean up this place." And she herself took Tej Kaur's shawl to wash it.

Chet Singh looked on, quite astonished. How had a minor mistake committed by her son melted this angry domineering woman like wax? If only she had blurted out angry insulting words, he would have beheaded both mother and son! So much for the Sandhu Sardarni!

Meanwhile Tej Kaur took her shawl from her kudamani and spoke sharply to her son. "Get up! You seem to have settled down her quite comfortably... Haven't we had enough here?"

Shingara's mother tried her best to persuade her to stay, cajoling her but it was in vain. Even Chet Singh joined her. "Don't be so furious. So what if your son has dropped milk on the floor? Please do have something to drink at least."

"Bhaiya ji, we have had much milk to drink. And more than enough to eat!" She retorted looking daggers at everyone. Then, pulling her son by his arm, she stormed out of the haveli. Actually Tej Kaur had eaten nothing since morning. Her eyes were flashing fire. She was ready to tear them to pieces and eat them.

The situation seemed to have gone out of control. 'If one party becomes unreasonable and shameless,' she thought, 'the other should try to behave with dignity at least. Our kudams are behaving like sweepers and scavengers! We almost came to blows....' She just wanted to get out of there at the earliest.

Unseasonal dark thunderclouds loomed overhead threatening a terrible storm but a wayward wind blew them ahead, scattering them.

Mother and son arrived.

All the members of the haveli were waiting for them with bated breath. Puro's heart was sinking with anxiety. She wondered what bombshell would explode with Bebe's arrival. Eventually Sadhu Singh broke the long uneasy silence.

"What have you achieved, Bhabi?"

Tej Kaur glared at everybody. Then, with her nose up in the air, she spat out.

"Damn all! I achieved nothing! They are a bunch of no-good uncivilised nomads. My God! I've never seen such a worthless lot. They have absolutely no decency! They are born shameless and rude. They have no idea of politeness. No manners! 'Take twice the amount from us,' they had the cheek to say! Had I gone to beg alms? Dogs! They didn't even want to mention the stolen calf.... Sadhu! They might even have killed us, and in their own courtyard! At least then their true worth would have been known to everyone.... To beat up and kill their own son-in-law and his mother in their own home!" She paused for a moment to catch her breath and then continued: "You would have then brought back the corpses of mother and son. If you have the guts – and the strength – you will avenge the treatment given to your Bhabi and your nephew!"

Tej Kaur paused again but not for long. "Sadheya! God has saved us this time.... Come to think of it, it would have been far better if they had killed us. With the loss of two lives the whole matter would have ended. Now, heaven alone knows who all will have to be sacrificed. I knew it all along - your uncle was advised not to have a marriage alliance with the Virks! They are known to be thieves and to have not the least notion of courtesy...."

The haveli fell as silent as a graveyard. There was not a sound from any corner. Puro desperately wanted to know what had actually happened but she was too afraid to come forward and ask. She thought to herself: 'Oh! Shingara! What a brother! You have ruined the happy settled home of your younger sister. Now matters cannot be settled short of a death or two in the families. Who will dare cross Bebe? My God, take me away from all this! How can I stand to see it happen? My husband on one side, and my brother on the other! One of them will surely die....' Tears streamed down her cheeks and, quite unconsciously, she threw herself against the wall. Tej Kaur heard the thud of the impact before she saw her. She turned on Puro and shouted at her.

"Why are you trying to end your life in our house? To implicate us and blame us? Go! Go and die in the house of those rogues who were not ashamed to steal from their own sister's home."

"Bebe ji! I shall certainly die in my father's house," Puro responded sobbing loudly. "God will deliver me from this torture! I must surely have been born with bad karma – I must endure the fruits of my ignoble past deeds."

"Because of one person's wrongdoing, the entire family has to suffer! If you are the daughter of Virks, we too are all Sandhus.... We can jump to death if we have to. Things have gone too far. I could sense your father's intentions – he was about to cut off his son-in-law's head! Bibi, the real fire will rage now. Let us see what he does. Will Dalipa die, or Shingara?"

"Bebe! You are a respected senior member of the family, don't say such terrible things! Just pray that I die. That will still the hearts of both the families and cool them down. That is the only thing which will bring peace now."

Hearing this from her daughter-in-law Tej Kaur felt disarmed. And yet it was like receiving another blow from the Virks. All the arrows in her own quiver had been shot. All her tactics and efforts had been of no avail. She called out to Dalip Singh. "Dalipiye! I'm telling Puro to prepare for her departure. You, too, get ready. Go and leave her at her parents' door. She cannot be absorbed and adjusted in our family." And she thought to herself, 'I'll see now how great is the ego of that man, how much self-respect he has!'

"Look! Girl." Tej Kaur instructed Puro. "Pack your luggage. Take whatever you like. Your folks shouldn't point a finger and say that your mother-in-law turned you out without money or clothes."

"Bebe ji, if my husband becomes a stranger to me and I am turned out of my house, what use have I for any things?" Puro asked as she went up to Dalip Singh and entreated him. "Oh Sardar! Why kill me by inches, uprooting me in such a way? Better that you strangle me with your own hands! I'll leave a note saying that I am responsible for hanging myself and ending my life." Then, turning back towards her mother-in-law, Puro fell at her feet seeking mercy. Tej Kaur drew her feet back uttering these harsh bitter words – "Can God be so unjust? Can I have the daughter of thieves living in my house?" – and she left the room.

The whole village was aghast. What had happened between Tej Kaur and the Virk sardars became the talk of the town. People gathered under the big banyan tree to catch up with the latest development of this episode.

"Why, Jawan! I heard that her kudams sent Tej Kaur back empty-handed."

Bali brahmin took a deep draught from his zhari and replied, "They should have given her a send off on the back of an elephant! After all she had gone with great pomp and pride because she was the mother of their son-in-law."

"Oh Pandit! If daughters are born does it mean the parents must cater to every whim of the in-laws? That the boy's people can do exactly as they please? Have the girl's people no rights? What kind of justice is this! After all, the big gun had marched to them, the Bhangi's cannon for which sweepers and scavengers are fodder. She had gone to lay seige to the fort of the Virks. And the Virks vanquished her forever!" Ditt, the marassi, fumbled for fire from the cinders of his chillum and remarked, "Brother Baliram, if these people are Sandhus those are no less. They are Virk Sardars who had routed the barbarians completely in battle….."

"I tell you this whole thing is nothing but a matter of ego and pride. I've heard that Dalipa's father-in-law had offered four times the money! But our Sardarni is as obstinate as a mule who lashes out with his hind legs without moving an inch."

"But Dada, she is a woman with pride and self-respect. In any case it isn't wise to be so stubborn all the time."

Kheda, the barber, chipped in. "Dada, whatever happened was in bad taste. The Virks after all were the parents of a daughter. What would they have lost if they had given the calf back? Was it so important for them to keep the beast? The girl's parents should be a bit submissive."

"Go! Go and get busy shaving some chin or head," the bard stopped him short. "These are matters of affluent families. Those people are not barbers or marassis who go around singing like minstrels at the drop of a hat." He then lowered his voice and continued, "I have even heard that Dalipa's father-in-law would have finished off Dalipa but the Sardarni intervened and saved the situation. She saved him.... Now the Haveli of the Zaildars is on fire. They say the Sardarni is furious – she is fuming and frothing with rage."

Nobody interrupted. He sat back for a while and continued. "We are marassis, the people who know the secrets of the deepest dungeons of the earth. Our words are never hollow or meaningless. Take it from me. One or the other from either family will die. The Virks are a stubborn clan and the Sandhus have become banias. They even grow green chillies and onions for business!"

Bali brahmin sighed. "Well! May God look after us!" He picked up his zhari and prepared to leave. "It is already evening. Let us go and prepare our meals."

After he left, gradually the company dispersed.

Tej Kaur saw to it that her son and daughter-in-law were ready to leave the next morning before the sun rose. Two horses were saddled. Dalip mounted one, and Puro, wailing and weeping, clasping her child to her bosom, screamed before leaving, "Bebe ji, I'm leaving this prosperous home for good! Never to return. Please forgive for me my faults and mistakes."

Tej Kaur screwed up her nose at Puro's desperate cry and said coldly: "Ask your father's and brother's forgiveness! You are going back because of them."

In Ghummani the news spread fast that Chet Singh's son-in-law had come to return his daughter. The girl covered her face with both her hands, and sobbing loudly, she entered the haveli. Oh! God. Strange are your ways. Such a small matter has caused such a serious rift between the two families.

Pulling him by his arm, his mother-in-law tried to bring Dalip Singh inside the house. "Come, my good son," she begged him. "Have something to drink, you've travelled such a long distance." But he stood impassively at the doorway, outside the haveli, holding his horse's reins, and made sure he did not utter a word.

Puro stood inside clutching her little daughter in a tight embrace. She looked at her father, and then at her husband. Neither of them could think of what to say. Meanwhile, Chet Singh's father Bapu Budh Singh came out. His straight flowing white beard, his moustache twirled upwards into a sharp curved point, and under his turban the tight knot of his jooda were all proof that he was a real Virk. He gauged the whole situation instantly. Digging a peg in the ground he turned towards his daughter-in-law, "Look here, my girl! Why are you begging these worthless people?"

Turning to Dalip Singh he said curtly, "Now, young man. Get going. Leave this place. Whatever you have done to us is good. You have played with our honour. Insulted us. I'll take it that my granddaughter has become a widow and returned home. Where there are so many people it doesn't matter that there are two more mouths to feed. This mother and her little daughter will be well looked after. But now, since you have abandoned our daughter, get ready for the consequences! You have brought dishonour to our clan and, worse, you have insulted me personally. You will have to pay for this!"

All those who were standing there trembled with fear. What if Bapu ji hits Dalipa? A few blows would decimate him and no one would know what to do. Chet Singh took the initiative. He tugged at Dalipa's arm and said, "Now leave. Leave like a good boy.... We have had enough!"

Six months have passed since Puro returned to her parents. Though the initial tension had eased somewhat there remained in each camp a festering anxiety fanned by the tales people carried to the Sandhus about the Virks and tattle to the Virks about what was going on at the Sandhus. Every now and then passions would flare up in each camp but there was no head-on clash. They were not exactly free from anxiety but they couldn't put the matter aside. And neither clan was willing to relent. The bone of contention was the calf. The poor animal had become a symbol of the self-respect and prestige of both the families.

The following winter Bapu Budh Singh's elder brother, Bapu Jagat Singh, came to visit them. They were sitting in the sun on their charpais and Taya Jagat Singh heard the whole story. He turned towards all the members of the family and spoke.

"Oye, Budh Singh! You are the eldest and the wisest, and yet you are adding fuel to the fire. Your obstinacy is going to kill this poor girl! Listen to me, and be a man. Send Bibi Puro with me. I will go myself and take her back to her husband's house and settle matters with them. A parents' home can never be a permanent nest for a daughter, not even among kings and emperors."

"Bhaiya ji, we will accept whatever you say, undergo any punishment you decide. But returning the calf is out of the question!" Budh Singh replied.

The next day Shingara's mother made all the preparations for the departure of her daughter Puro with Bapu Jagat Singh. She loaded the bullock cart with all kinds of gifts. After all Puro was going to her in-laws' house after six long months. Two escorts were sent with them. One to look after the child and the other to bring back Puro's horse.

Sardarni Tej Kaur welcomed her kudam with full ceremony and warm hospitality, and he, in turn, humbly and with folded hands, entreated her to allow the girl in the house. He then returned to Ghummani the following day. Once again there was peace all around.

But it wasn't so. Tej Kaur couldn't sleep the whole night. She felt trapped. She had exhausted all her tactics. Had she sent the girl back with Sardar Jagat Singh Virk it would have been extremely insulting and arrogant. Though the matter had exploded so much yet things were back to square one.] It seemed to her that the Virks had got their way after all. They had bulldozed their way to reinstate their daughter and they had not returned the calf! She burned with indignation whenever she thought about it. She felt engulfed by flames. How could she possibly sleep peacefully under such circumstances?

Almost two months have gone by since Puro came back to her husband. The Virks were pleased. They had their way and saved face. And their daughter was happily settled once again.

Tej Kaur was seething inside. She had come to know that Puro was pregnant. But this was no obstacle for the proud Sardarni. She was acutely aware that not only in the eyes of their own village, but even in the opinion of the entire region, the Haveli of the Zaildars had been reduced to naught.

One day, early in the morning, Tej Kaur flew into a rage and her roaring voice was heard. She was telling Dalipa: "Take Puro to her parents' home, we are not going to keep her in our house."

Sadhu heard Bhabi's harsh voice full of anger and he came running. At that moment she was instructing him to return Puro to her parents – "We are not going to keep the Virk girl in our house" – just as though he had brought a wrong item from a shop and she was insisting that it be returned.

Sadhu Singh stood before Bhabi with folded hands and pleaded: "Bhabi, I beseech you in the name of Baba Nanak, don't torture me any more. Don't drag my name through mud, don't insult me! Why are you bent on making me a sinner? As it is we have had enough. Don't drag our humiliation through the whole area! I curse the day when I bought the calf for sixty rupees.... Since then it has turned out to be Yama for both the families. Let Bibi stay on, in this, her home! Just let her be, Bhabi! Oh! God! Where should I drown myself....?"

"Sadheya, you stay where you are.... It is women who drown themselves. A jat's son and you are talking of killing yourself over such a trivial matter? Pick up your sword! Go to the Virks and get back the calf. Only then will I be assured that at least one lion son was born to the Sandhus. Let the haveli get destroyed, let there be a bloody fight! I cannot have the daughter of thieves live here.... I don't care about people; they are like dogs – they will wag their tongues but they will stop barking when they are tired. Neither my sons, nor my devars or nephews have ever stolen or robbed anything. No one can point a finger at them – they are decent sons of decent families. Honest people. Had Dalipa done what Shingara did I would have ripped his skin off his bones or else you wouldn't call me the daughter of Gill sardars. Don't you know the saying, 'Don't kill the thief, kill the thief's mother so she doesn't give birth to another thief'? And here you are! Standing before me with folded hands like a marassi! What kind of a Sandhu are you...!"

Dalip refused to take Puro back to her parents. But his younger brother, a few inches taller than him and more robust, agreed.

Weeping and wailing, Puro once again stood on the threshold of her parents' home. Her mother wept bitterly on seeing her. Beating her breast with both hands she lamented screaming loudly: "Just look! They are torturing my poor innocent, tender-as-a-flower daughter... killing her by inches... driving her to death, this family of tigers!" Hearing the screams of Puro's mother, people gathered not only from the haveli but from outside too. Dalip's brother sprang onto his horse, took the reins of the other in his hand, and vanished.

Once again pandemonium was let loose. Bapu Budh Singh kept wringing his hands and shouting, "You dogs! Why the hell did you let the boy escape? You should have grabbed both the horses and beaten the bastard black and blue and thrown him into the lock up. And we would have dealt with whoever else comes the same way! So far they haven't been able to harm us, but now those sons of bitches have done the worst they could!"

Budh Singh was furious with his brother Jagat Singh. He fumed inwardly: If you hadn't intervened this would not have happened. We spent two thousand rupees to settle our girl with her husband...they absorbed it silently. Only six months have passed and they are burning a pyre in front of our house again!

Chet Singh somehow managed to take Budh Singh, who was still brandishing his stick in rage, inside. After some time all was quiet. Puro, half dead, stretched out on the floor with her little daughter clinging to her bosom. Every member of the family was burning within like corpses in a crematorium. It seemed as though the days of doom were approaching fast.

Once again there was a deathly silence in both the households. It was like the peace that descends when a dear one finally passes away after a long protracted illness.

Some months later, at twilight, Tej Kaur was finishing her chores in the kitchen before turning in. She had collected the milk and was just putting it away when there was a loud knock on the door. Gopal Singh and Tej Kaur both ran to open it. In the semi-darkness they saw a stranger on horseback. Without dismounting he said: "Sardar ji, I am from Ghummani. Bibi Puro gave birth to a son. But it was God's will...both mother and son have passed away. The cremation will take place in the morning."

Tej Kaur felt the earth slipping from under her feet and she haltingly begged the departing man with folded hands: "My good man! Look! Look at my folded hands, and tell the Virk sardars to wait. Tell them that I am begging them, with folded hands, not to cremate my daughter-in-law and grandson until we reach. We are on our way...."

As soon as the messenger's back was turned, the Sardarni lamented in a loud sing-song voice: "Listen everybody! My moon-faced grandson has died along with his mother! And we didn't even see him...no one thought of showing him to her in-laws! What a terrible fate!"

The whole haveli assembled. The entire village assembled. And Sardarni Tej Kaur wailed louder, holding her head in her hands and rocking back and forth. Her dupatta slipped to fall on the ground, and her hair opened to fall on her shoulders. She continued to wail. "Oh! Why didn't death strike me? Why didn't I die! Such a happy family is ruined...."

Moments later she suddenly stopped crying. A few seconds later she said to the old barber's wife, Buddhi Nayan, and Jeevan, the marassan, "The village is still awake. Inform everybody that we will leave for Ghummani before daybreak. Both of you get ready and come." Then she began ordering everyone: "Sadheya, Dalipa, saddle the horses! I cannot wait for a single moment any more." She continued giving instructions. The whole haveli bustled with activity as people ran about doing whatever was necessary.

Soon relatives and friends collected in front of the haveli, some on horses or mares, some on bicycles. They whispered in each other's ears but none had the courage to even breathe loudly in the presence of the Sardarni.

This caravan of forty or fifty people reached the village of the Virks as day dawned. The horses were left in the care of servants to be tethered near the well. And Sardarni Tej Kaur led the way, flaunting her silk shawl. Just as she turned into the street near the haveli, she looked up at the heavens and let forth a shrieking lament.

"My God! Listen! I have been robbed in broad daylight...the lion son of the Sandhus has gone! Snatched away... what did he see of the world? Oh! Oh! My lion grandson has been killed because of their stubbornness!"

Spit dribbled out of her mouth as she let out scream after scream. Her shawl fell off her shoulders. The two corpses lay on a bed in the outermost room, wrapped in white sheets, their heads covered. The Sardarni uncovered Puro's face and, kissing it again and again, said: "Oh look! My loving girl was like sandalwood... see how they made her suffer. They didn't look after her...she died of neglect! Oye! Rishia, see who has come!

My lion, my child! You'll never see your youth.... But see who has come – all your uncles, your chachas and tayas." And she beat her head against the wooden leg of the charpai. A fountain of blood gushed from her head and spread all over the white sheet covering Puro. The people close by managed to pull her away, their arms around her shoulders, and take her aside and she continued to wail: "No, nothing has happened to me. I'm left behind to suffer! My very life has gone away, taking her son with her!"

Blood was still oozing out of the bandage on the Sardarni's head as she waited for the men-folk to return from the cremation grounds. She was still squatting on the floor hugging her granddaughter.

The maids and servants were busy preparing food for everyone. Puro's mother held Tej Kaur's hand and tried to comfort her. "Bibi, no one has the power to avert what has happened. It was God's will. Please get up and have a sip of water.... You haven't eaten since last night and you've travelled ten kos."

Puro's chachi was also entreating her. But Sardarni Tej Kaur merely looked at her coldly and, holding her granddaughter in her arms, said commandingly: "What are you looking at me for? Come, Sandhu sardars. Let's go home. Our relationship with this household broke a year ago. We will eat or drink nothing here."

The horses were brought to the entrance of the haveli. Tej Kaur walked out of the courtyard to her bay horse and said to the boy holding the bridle, "Here. Hold my daughter for a moment." She put her foot into the stirrup and swung herself into the saddle. Turning to the boy she stretched out her arms and said, "Give me my child."

Tej Kaur settled the girl into her lap and held her in a firm embrace as she dug her heels into the haunches of the horse. It set off.

She did not turn around to see who all were standing there watching her go.

THE WEIGHT OF THE WORLD

Kulwant Singh Virk

The village of Thhati Khara was quite close to Amritsar, on the main road. The way Man Singh was travelling there, happily, a place far, far away would also seem near. Though dusk had fallen, and the horse pulling the tonga was tired, he was not unduly worried.

Man Singh was a soldier on leave. Thhati Khara is where his dear friend Karam Singh's home was. The close friendships forged in the army cannot be formed anywhere else. At first they were together in the Regimental Centre and now their battalion was posted on active duty in the Burma front. Karam Singh had joined earlier and was a Havildar while Man Singh was still on the first rung of the ladder as a Naik.

The outstanding quality of Karam Singh was his gregariousness, his gentle nature and the ability to communicate easily and sweetly with people. There were others too from the

---

Dharti hethla bulad. Translated by Jasjit Mansingh

same village in the army, a taciturn lot. When they went home on leave the extent of their communication was limited to a greeting – Wahe Guru di Fateh – while when Karam Singh went home the number of people who came to bathe at the well would swell. In winter people would stay up late, braving the cold till the clay fireplace over which maize and other grain was roasted lost its warmth, listening to the anecdotes Karam Singh related. In his regiment he was quite famous for his marksmanship. During shooting competitions he would invariably get the bull's eye; it was almost as though someone had pulled the bullet through the centre of the target manually. In this war his incredible aim and steadiness enabled him to bring down Japanese soldiers hiding behind trees at a far distance when others could see nothing but branches. This is how he avenged the death of his comrades who fell to Japanese snipers and assuaged the rage that swept through his platoon. Where a spray of machine gun fire was ineffective, a single bullet fired by Karam Singh found its mark and accomplished the job. He was becoming older now but even so when he worked out on the bars during gymnastics, the spectators would watch spellbound. He was like a man possessed.

During wartime of course all that was stopped. So were a lot of other things. There was no parade, no marching smartly wearing stiffly starched uniforms while the band played. There was no bazaar nearby where they could go to relax in mufti. There was nobody from their village, or even their district, with whom they could let their hair down. When Man Singh's turn came for leave, Karam Singh was upset. If he too had leave they could have gone together, had a good time, and returned together.

From Amrtisar Choohadkala was not far, hardly a distance of 50 koh [about 60 miles], but they were worlds apart and known by distinct names. The former area had been long established and was called Majha while the latter was in the region known as Baar and had only recently been settled. Since it was difficult to get leave these days, occasionally one or two would be fortunate enough to go rather in the way that medals for bravery are won by only a few, sometimes.

When Man Singh was leaving, as he was about to get into the military truck, Karam Singh said to him: "You must also visit my people. When they know you have come from me, it will almost seem to them that they are with me. When you return, having met them, and tell me how things are with them it will feel as though I myself have visited!"

Trying to spur him into making the visit, Karam Singh threw in some additional bait. He asked: "Have you ever been there before?"

"No. I've passed through Amritsar but never gone beyond."

"There are many gurudwaras there – Taran Taaran, Khadur Sahib, Goindwal. Pay your respects there and also visit my home. I'll write to tell them you're coming...."

That is how it was, a few days before his leave finished, that he was sitting in a tonga on his way to his friend Karam Singh's village.

"Bapu ji, I'm Man Singh from Chhoohadkala." Man Singh announced to the old man sitting in the verandah at the entrance of Karam Singh's home.

"Welcome. Blessings be to you. Come and sit down."

Man Singh entered and sat down on the charpai. It seemed as though the old man was a bit uncomfortable with his presence. At first he had looked around vaguely but then he sat quietly with eyes downcast.

Man Singh did not belong to that area and he was a bit taken aback at this formal reception. Perhaps the old man himself was a stranger.

"Are you Karam Singh's father?" He asked since he had fully expected to be received warmly and with much affection.

"Yes, I am. This is his home."

"Didn't he write to you about me...?"

"Yes, he wrote that you would be coming to meet us." And he got up and walked away towards the courtyard. He untied the young female calf from one peg and retied her to another, then stroking her body he put his hand next to her mouth so she could lick it. He disappeared inside to announce Man Singh's arrival and to ask for tea to be prepared. Then, as though he was reluctant to return to the verandah, he wandered over to the mare also tied in the courtyard. He turned over the fodder in front of her, got some more gram and mixed it in, and then finally turned around and came back. He seemed to be a little more in control now and not quite so vague. He looked towards Man Singh and then all around.

"Where's Jaswant Singh?" Man Singh knew that Jaswant Singh was Karam Singh's younger brother.

Karam Singh's mother, who came in with the tea just then, answered, "He'll just be back, he has gone to fetch some fodder."

"Bebe ji, Sat Sri Akal!" Man Singh greeted the old woman with a sparkling smile in his eyes.

The old woman's lips moved as though she would say something but no words came. Man Singh took the small round vessel of tea and the steel bowl from her and she went back inside.

"What kind of people are these?" Man Singh thought in astonishment, feeling quite disturbed. But then having come to someone's home he could hardly leave right away. "Well. I'll stay one night and then go," he decided.

Later in the evening, when Jaswant Singh returned, the atmosphere lightened and there was some conversation.

"Karam Singh's marksmanship has become quite famous there in the Burma war. He just has to pull the trigger once, and in the blink of an eye a Japanese falls. And we, walking along with him, have no idea how he spots them!"

Man Singh stopped expecting that they would ask lots of questions about the war. He was bursting with stories he wanted to tell but no one spoke. They sat in silence for some time until the old man asked Jaswant Singh:

"When is it our turn for water?"

"It will be at three in the morning, day after tomorrow."

Hearing 'three in the morning' Man Singh started off again.

He was so full of warmth for his friend that he wanted to talk about him to his hearts content.

"I remember another thing... How Karam Singh managed to avoid the last night watch...! He is extremely lazy about getting up in the morning, he is always the last one to get up there."

Even then no one seemed to be interested.

Then food was served. A lot of trouble had been taken to prepare it. As he ate, Jaswant fanned him. He felt reassured that they were not ignoring him deliberately.

While they were still eating, Karam Singh's little son toddled into the room and came up to Man Singh's charpai. If he couldn't talk about Karam Singh to anyone else he could at least talk to his son! Man Singh picked him up and held him in his arms.

"Oye! Do you want to go to your father? If you do, come with me. It rains a lot there, you can play in the rain."

Hearing this the old man felt as though a dart had been driven through his heart. "Come and get the boy," he called out quite sharply, "and keep him there. Let us at least eat in peace." Bebe came and took the boy away.

Man Singh began to feel absolutely stifled in the house. He wanted to cut short his visit and return as soon as he could. He would start out the next day, he thought and asked, "How far is Tarn Taaran from here?"

"About four koh."

"I suppose one can get a tonga early in the morning?"

"Don't worry about tongas. We'll send Jaswant with you. Both you brothers can go together and pay your respects."

Man Singh agreed. Jaswant Singh was not such a tight-lipped fellow.

But as he walked beside Man Singh, he too was quite silent. Even when they passed friends he would merely greet them from a distance and walk on while Man Singh wished they would stop and have a little conversation. It was not likely that he would be visiting here again.

"Karam Singh has really made a name for himself in the army. Why didn't you join the army?" Man Singh asked Jaswant trying to draw him out.

Jaswant shrank into himself as a thief would if he were caught red handed. After a while he answered, "Is one in the army not enough!"

They happened to be passing a field of fodder and Jaswant changed the subject. "How tall have the stalks grown where you come from?"

"Man high. They look like soldiers standing to attention." But he wasn't at all interested in small talk, all he wanted to do was talk about his friend.

When they returned to the village Man Singh thought he should go back to his own home. If he caught the night train from Amritsar he would reach early the next morning. Even though all of them had been very courteous and looked after him well he was very disappointed with the whole trip. Even now tea was being prepared for him inside while he sat by himself in the verandah.

Outside in the street he could see the postman coming along, his bag slung over his shoulder. It looked as though he would continue straight past but then he stopped at the verandah, came in and sat down on the charpai.

"What have you brought?"

"What is there to bring…? There is just this pension, poor Karam Singh."

"Karam Singh's pension…! Has Karam Singh been killed?"

"My good man! The whole neighbourhood is deep in sorrow, and you, sitting in his own home are asking if Karam Singh has been killed? The letter came fifteen days ago."

Shocked, Man Singh's breathing became laboured. He felt that his forehead was held in a tight clamp which was only loosened once the tears coursed from his eyes. Karam Singh's father, who was still inside, and his little son too were crying.

The old man saw the postman sitting there and he understood that there was nothing more to hide. There was no need now to carry that burden. The weight of restraint and composure he had endured for the whole day finally lifted as his tears flowed. They sat close, next to each other, and allowed their tears to fall freely.

Finally, Man Singh said, "Why didn't you tell me when I came?"

"Just. You have come on leave ... and we didn't want to ruin that for you. We thought you would find out anyhow when you went back to the battalion after your leave. Leave is so precious for a soldier, as precious for you as it was for Karam Singh, perhaps more. The people of Baar are not conditioned to hardship, for them even a little difficulty seems too much. But we, we couldn't even hide this from you. We spoilt your leave."

On his way back Man Singh saw the villages of Majha where the old man had been born and bred. The landscape was dotted with forts in which the villages nestled. In the open were graves and tombs which spoke of the battles earlier generations had fought against the invaders who came to subjugate India. Everything told the story of war, of living and dying. Man Singh remembered another story, that of the bull which held up the entire world on its head. He felt as though Karam Singh's father was like that bull, weighed down with sorrow but he still took upon himself the burdens of others.

II

A MIRACLE

Jaswant Singh Virdi

I don't remember which day of the week it was, but the date was the seventeenth or eighteenth of August. All around Wagah there had been an orgy of killing. The murdering mobs had surrounded Khan Sahib's daughter in the choubara, the room on the roof of his house.

For two days and two nights the girl had used the room like a fortress. The people were armed with knives and daggers. But that brave girl had a pistol and a large quantity of bullets. She used the bullets not to kill people but to defend herself. She used the pistol only when it was necessary. Thus had she saved herself for two days. The mob was quite surprised.

Her father had built the house after his retirement just at the point where Panj Pir Bazaar started. That was in 1946 and by March 1947 small bands of people had started their mischief and some incidents had taken place. But the house had been

---

Karamat. Translated by Jasjit Mansingh

built and it wasn't easy to leave it and go. Anyhow, there was still a little wooden board hanging outside: House for Sale.

But there were no buyers. No one knew what the future would bring. Sometimes there were rumours that the boundary for the partition of Punjab would be at the river Sutlej, but it then slid up to Wagah.

We were very young then, barely about fifteen years old, and we didn't know much about the reasons for the unrest. We knew though that S.D.O. Khan's daughter was besieged in the choubara and that she was firing in self defence. What would happen to her? We were extremely interested in the outcome… not only we, everyone was.

Huge mobs had descended on Raunak Bazaar and Sheikha Bazaar to loot and the bazaars and lanes were strewn with corpses. But the daughter of Khan Sahib, in the prime of youth, held her ground, holding the mobs at bay.

But the third day was full of cruelty.

On this day some people stormed the chaubara and managed to break down the heavy teak door and were able to drag the young woman out. They had guessed that she had run out of bullets. If she had had more ammunition it would have been at least another two days before they could force it open.

As they pulled her out they taunted her angrily: "Did you think you could have made a tunnel through the ground and escape from Wagah?"

She was not perturbed. It was almost as though she knew what was about to happen to her.

We thought that either the police or the army would save her from the mob. But there were no signs of any police there, nor for that matter of the army. There was only the mob milling around and there was the fair, tall and lissome girl whom they forced to walk ahead of them. She was defenceless and they were armed. They were also full of anger. However, since nobody had been killed or wounded by her bullets, they had not killed her as soon as they got their hands on her. But their intent was perhaps worse. It was written clearly on their faces: "We will torture you in such a way that you'll not forget it easily...."

'The daughter of S.D.O. Khan of Panj Pir has been captured.' The news spread like wildfire. The women were very upset. But the men pressed forward eagerly towards Pir Panjal Chowk as though some very special entertainment had been arranged there.

My mother followed me to try and stop me. Many people from Gobindgarh were also headed there and at their insistence she turned back. She kept repeating to herself: "The poor thing, Khan Sahib's daughter.... Who knows what lies in store for her...? Why have people become so heartless...?"

In our minds there was a kind of expectant excitement as we wondered what the mob would do to her. It was this immense curiosity that lent our feet wings.

We used to live then close to the railway station in Gobindgarh and people from this locality had been very active in the city - plundering and killing. Many had looted the homes of Muslims and filled their own homes. Overnight they had become rich. Specially with household goods. But books and papers had been abandoned, scattered in the lanes of the bazaars.

Suddenly we received a big shock. There, in front of us, was the girl. Stark naked. There was not a bit of cloth on her body. Her hair had been cut, and for a moment we wondered if it was she. But the rest of her body left no doubt in the minds of the onlookers because behind her stood some men armed with swords, unpityingly, guarding her. There was no way she could escape. The thought then triggered another: 'Why are those people guarding her?'

For two whole days she had fought the mob. She lost because her ammunition finished. Had she even had any food to eat or water to drink?

Mother used to tell us: "When your brother was working on the Jamuna bridge, the girl's father, Khan Sahib, was there too as an S.D.O. He had three wives. He built this house for one of them. Your brother even went to meet Khan Sahib.... The poor girl...."

Remembering what she said, I was filled with compassion. Our father was employed by the Station Masrer. I felt that there was a deep connection here.

Our hearts were beating fast.

At Sinmaiyan Chowk some men with daggers stopped us. "There is no need to go further. The procession is coming this way."

"But why is that poor thing being subjected to being paraded thus?"

"The other side of Wagah the same thing was done with our young girls...."

"Was this girl responsible for their abduction?"

"Born yesterday and yet you boys have such long tongues!"

"Our father also works in the Railways," I told them. "And she too is the daughter of an officer in the Railways, an S.D.O. isn't she?"

"So? What is that to you?"

"Nothing. But let her go." And we pressed on.

We went a little further and some other people stopped us. "Don't go any further."

"Why?"

"It is forbidden to look upon a naked woman."

"Then why has she been stripped?"

"For revenge.... REVENGE! Get it?"

The people who had stopped us were huge men, tall and fierce. We could not have taken them on. I thought: 'If they should come to know that we have hidden Muslim girls at home, perhaps they will knife me...." Best to be quiet. Soldiers had come to escort the girls from our home but the people had not liked that at all. If the mobs had found them they would surely have killed us too.

The procession had come very close. Looking at her she didn't seem to be a Muslim. Everything about her was like....as if....just like any other woman. Her form and colour....her body...and everything else....

I looked at her closely and then I I found I couldn't look at her again. It was as though her body was full of thorns, thorns that pierced our eyes. How strange!

We were thinking: 'How is it possible that people took off her clothes but then attached these thorns to her body?'

I have never heard anywhere that a body can grow thorns. Yes. The thorns were really in the lusting eyes of the onlookers.

Was this just some foolishness, or was it something else? I took off my turban, quickly stepped forward and wrapped it around that girl's body. I was thinking: 'This gift of the Lord, Guruji, has today been put to good use....'

But my action caused a commotion in the crowd. She too had been startled. She had opened her eyes and looked at me. I think she had said to me: 'Oh honourable man! Allah will bless you.'

She herself was caught in this terrible misfortune but in spite of that she had blessed me. Right then, I don't know from where, a knife whistled through the air coming directly towards me. But before it could strike me, the girl had stepped in front of me and the knife struck her in the middle of the chest, right next to the heart... where it was beating....

"Ya Allah!" she cried out and she fell down. A line of blood trickled down from her chest soaking my turban and turning it blood red.

I think she believed that Allah would come to her rescue, and there would surely be some miracle. It was afternoon and the August sun was hot and the light blazing. The faces of the people there looked awestruck.

Wrapped in my blood soaked turban that young woman, on the threshold of the prime of life, lay in a heap on the street and through the hubbub and noise of the collected crowd I heard her say as she looked at me: "Don't worry about me, Brother."

My body is slightly built and not too robust. I don't know how I had done what I did. Whenever I recall that sight I begin to tremble and my heart begins to beat faster.

I remember that those people beat me up but they didn't beat me to death.

I remember that the words of that dying girl lingered in my ears:

"Oh honourable man! Allah will bless you."

HUNGER

Krishen Singh Dhody

It was the silver jubilee week of "The Blood of the Lover" running at Nishaat cinema. The film had drawn a packed house for every showing during the preceding twenty-five weeks. That was not surprising as everyone has, at one time or the other, been in love. Everyone loved the film because they found their own life-story projected on the screen. The producer decided to celebrate the success by taking out a triumphal procession through the streets of the city. The publicity campaign was entrusted to a contractor, Sundar Singh.

Sundar Singh was a pleasant man of about forty-five. He lived in a house close to Nishaat. He lived alone because he did not have a relative in the world to share his home. He had employed a fifteen-year-old lad, Bachana Singh, to cook his meals for him. Bachana Singh gave his master the morning and the evening meal and spent the rest of the day parading through the streets

---

Translated by Khushwant Singh

sandwiched between cinema placards. For this he was paid Rs 25 a month, all of which he gave to his widowed mother who lived in a refugee encampment.

The procession of the film "The Blood of the Lover" started from the cinema hall at 8 a.m. Sundar Singh wore a bright red turban with starched plumes flaunting in the air. He carried a flag in his hand and ran up and down the procession shouting instructions. Heading the procession was Master Raja Lal's brass band. Following the band was a truck bearing mammoth portraits of the stars of the film; one picture showed a fountain of blood pouring out of the heart of the lover and falling at the feet of his sweetheart. Following the truck were a row of bullock carts decorated with hoardings. Following the bullock carts were sandwich-men. And last of all came little urchins carrying sticks with placards stuck to them. Amongst the urchins was Bachana Singh.

Bachana Singh wore a clean shirt and pyjama; he had even polished his shoes. But there was no sign of joy in his face. He trudged on silently in the last rank with his eyes downcast and an age-old melancholy in his drooping visage. And there was his employer, Sundar Singh, strutting about with the airs of a Field Marshall, now commanding the band to play another air; now commanding the cart drivers to keep in line; and again bellowing at the little boys to march in step.

It was a grand spectacle.

Although the procession had been organised by the rich, the people who marched in it were poor – the poor who had agreed to tramp through dusty streets to be able to fill their bellies. Anyone pausing to see their pale, emaciated faces would have concluded that the procession was intended to advertise poverty – poverty which had celebrated a hundred thousand silver and golden jubilees.

The procession entered the city. It went along the main street, the Mall, past the city's biggest bakery. The bakery bore a large signboard picturing a giant loaf of bread with the legend 'Delbis'. Bachana Singh's eyes fell on the picture and his mouth filled with saliva, and he ran his tongue over his lips. He stopped in front of the bakery and stood entranced, gaping at the board. Sundar Singh's harsh voice pierced through his dream: "Oi! Bachana! Oi, you son of a witch! Keep moving."

Bachana Singh ran to catch up with the rest but his thoughts stayed behind with the loaf of bread. He marched on with the procession his mind stuck to the hoarding. His feet went one way and his heart another. He pondered over the hard life he led.

Bachana Singh got up at six every morning to give his master breakfast consisting of tea, toast cut out of a small loaf of Delbis, and half a pat of butter. Sundar Singh used up all the butter and left only the crusts of the toasts for his servant, and Bachana Singh washed these down with his own cup of tea. Bachana Singh longed for the day when he would eat a whole loaf of Delbis, and have a whole pat of butter. Since he gave his wages to his mother, there was nothing to spare for luxuries such as these. Once when Sundar Singh had felt a little under the weather, he had taken only one toast and given the rest of the loaf to his servant. Bachana still cherished the memory of that day and prayed that his master would again be indisposed and the entire loaf and the pat of butter would be left to his share.

The picture in the bakery made him so ravenously hungry that he imagined himself swallowing the entire loaf in one gulp.

After breakfast Sundar Singh used to stroke his paunch and repeat: "Wahe Guru. Wahe Guru. Sache Pasha! I thank Thee, thou Emperor True, a hundred thousand times. Guru Gobind, Lord of the Plumes, all that Thy humble servant gets is but Thy gift. Thou givest and Thy humble servant's hunger is appeased." And then he would emit a long, satisfied belch.

Bachana heard these words of thanksgiving every morning. How strange, he wondered that the Sache Pasha should give to some and not to others! That he should give Sundar Singh a whole loaf with butter every day and to him only leftover crusts! And he would resume his breakfast of dry crusts dipped in tea.

Sometimes Bachana asked himself why he had never thanked the Guru, the True Emperor. So one day he blurted out: "Great Guru. Sache Pasha! For what I have received I thank Thee a hundred thousand times!" Immediately after he had uttered the words he felt a little silly. What had he to thank the Guru for? Just for the dry crusts of bread? The thanks were due from Sundar Singh because he got the whole loaf and butter every day. If he, Bachana, gave thanks for the crusts, that's all the Guru would ever give him!

Once Sundar Singh went off toast for a few days. He began to take milk instead for his breakfast. Poor Bachana was deprived of even his scraps of toast. It is no wonder that the mere picture of a loaf of bread made him drool. He resolved to buy the bread and butter, but where would the money come from?

When he returned home after parading the streets, he was

very tired. His limbs ached, and the longing for bread and butter gnawed at his insides. His master, Sundar Singh, came back, changed into a suit and left to go to a reception given by the producer of "The Blood of the Lover".

Bachana Singh had no means of raising a loan; he had asked his companions on the parade to give him eight annas but no one would lend him the money. Perhaps they were as hard up as he. Or did they suspect that he would never be able to return the loan? Bachana tried to get a loaf and butter from the restaurant at the cinema but that also failed. Sundar Singh had given instructions that nothing was to be given on credit to his servant. Bachana Singh, hungry, lay down on his charpoy.

Before he fell asleep, Bachana said a short prayer – his heart was too full for more. He hadn't asked for a million rupess, or motor cars, or bungalows. Only a small loaf of bread and half a pat of butter. Even that was denied him! He prayed fervently. "Great Guru! Sache Pasha! I have forsaken others and come to your door. People say you are the Great Giver. I too have seen your generosity towards the proprietor of Nishaat cinema and to the contractor Sundar Singh. But why don't you give me and a hundred thousand others like me? Who else can we turn to? If you really are the Great Giver, then give your servant a loaf of bread. Otherwise I will conclude that you are the Guru of the chosen few and I shall find a new Guru of my own." Praying, his eyes closed and he drifted off.

He awoke late at night with an eerie feeling. His room was filled with a strange effulgence. A bright glittering figure dismounted from a horse and entered his room. A white hawk fluttered on his hand. Of course! It was Guru Gobind himself! Bachana jumped up and bowed his head at the Guru's feet and then offered the Guru his humble three-legged stool. The Guru embraced Bachana.

"My son. You thought of me in your prayers!"

"Yes, Father." Bachana replied folding the palms of his hands and dropping his eyes.

"Why did you think of me, son?" the Guru asked with utmost kindness.

"Sache Pasha! You know the innermost secrets of our hearts. You know of my suffering!"

"Son, ask what you wish and it will be granted."

"Give me a small loaf of Delbis and half a pat of butter," Bachana blurted out smacking his lips.

"A loaf of Delbis and half a pat of butter! Four and three – that is only seven annas worth per day! Son, know the status of the One who gives and then ask. Ask for happiness in this life and in the life to come. Ask for dominion over the globe and I shall grant it to you. I can make you King of the three worlds!"

"No. No, my Lord! I do not want dominion or power. It was different in your age; today kings' heads roll in the dust and are kicked about by common people. All I need is a loaf of bread. And many who are as poor as I also need bread. I do not wish to own a kingdom but I also do not want to spend a lifetime in hunger and want. Just appease my hunger in this life and let us not worry about the life hereafter."

"You will get all you want and quite soon. In the life to come you will have everything in full measure. I will have to come back to this world again – not to save India from the perils of a foreign invasion but to give every Indian bread and butter. Wait for my return."

"Sache Pasha! I have waited long. Don't take too much time....come as soon as you can."

"I will not be long."

The effulgent figure remounted the horse and vanished.

"Oi! Bachania! Get up, you lazy lout! It is almost afternoon and you are still in bed! Get up and get my Delbis and butter."

Bachana had gone to bed very late, and then there was that strange dream. When he heard the word 'Delbis', he rose with a start still in his dream world.

"Sache Pasha! You have really come? And sooner than you promised! Where is my Delbis and my pat of butter?"

Sundar Singh looked at the boy quizzically. "Oi! Who do you think you are talking to? You didn't drug yourself with hashish, did you...? Do I get breakfast for you, or you for me? Get moving, you sluggard! And get my Delbis and butter."

"Soon, very soon, someone there is going to get Delbis and butter for me...."

Then Bachana opened his eyes. Sundar Singh stood over him, glowering. Quickly Bachana shut his eyes and stretched out on the charpoy again.

Sundar Singh lifted the charpoy from one end and titled it. Bachana rolled off and fell flat on his face on the floor.

HER LAST CRIES

Baldev Singh

When I had composed my face into a suitable expression of sadness, greeted the crowd of mourners sitting on durries and joined them shyly I saw that Bhagwan Kaur's dead body was lying on a charpai in the courtyard. Because of the heat and humidity big and small pieces of ice had been placed around it so it would not decompose. The courtyard was kutcha and water from the melting ice had collected under the charpai and the area around it turning it into slushy mud. Four or five women, or perhaps they were girls – I couldn't make out because they had their faces covered – were sitting around the charpai, their heads resting on the wooden frame, weeping. From among the group of women sitting a little further away one or two were keening loudly.

Besides the atmosphere of mourning, it was also extremely hot. The poor birds, their mouths open and their tongues hanging

---

Jaandi vaar diyan haakaan. Translated by Tara Meenakshi Sekhri out, were searching for shelter in the shade.

Cold drinking water was passed around frequently to the assembled mourners. Bhagwan Kaur's husband, Bohad Singh, wearing a yellow patka around his head, sat in one corner. The elders of the village and his close relatives sat close to him. Bohad Singh was remembering and recounting incidents from Bhagwan Kaur's life and telling them what happened in her last moments and how she died, stopping every now and then to wipe the tears from his eyes.

Bohad Singh's eldest son, Gurchetan, was sitting next to me. He was now the sarpanch of the village. I inched closer to him and asked, as is customary, in a soft whisper, "What happened to Tai ji?"

"She was quite well, except for fever for a few days. Day before yesterday she was very out of sorts. Yesterday we took her to the doctor in the city. He said that the fever had affected her brain but there was no cause to worry.... Half the medicines he gave are still lying there. And then this morning she died!"

"Was she ever sick like this before?"

"No, never. She never even had a headache," he replied proudly.

"How old was she?"

"Quite old I suppose..." He thought for a while and then said firmly, "She would have been at least seventy."

"That's no age at all! People of that generation are quite active even at ninety...." I sympathised.

"That's what was so surprising. She'd never been ill! I've never known her to have fever, or even heard her coughing. If she had any problems she never said anything to us. Nor have we ever seen her laid up in bed. And now, she got ill and was gone in a matter of days.... Just can't believe it! Nor can the neighbours or our relatives.... Whomever we informed on the phone was absolutely stunned..." Gurchetan stopped, choked with emotion.

In the courtyard the women continued with their intermittent keening. When they wiped the tears from their eyes they would also mop the perspiration on their brows. And they would look around to see who else was there. Which neighbours, which daughter-in-law or which mother-in-law had come, and who was wearing an inappropriate, a coloured, dupatta grabbed in a hurry. They would look disapprovingly and, at the same time, manage to display their own ornaments.

Where the men sat it was not as noisy as the women's group though conversations were going on there as well. The elders were philosophising about life and death. One of them was crying copiously and saying: "In vain do human beings carry on about me and mine, get agitated and anxious. Today, here, all notions of me and mine end. Just see how this jathedarni of such a well-respected family lies here now amidst slabs of ice. People will remember her for as long as it takes to reach the cremation ground. That is what will happen to all of us. But we forget it even while returning from the cremation and again the clamour of 'yours' and 'mine' starts...!

The teacher was holding forth. Another person who seemed to be a government official was talking about the inadequacies of the government. He kept returning to the same point: "The policies of the government will reduce the Jat to poverty."

As the relatives arrived, whether close or distant, the men, looking duly sorrowful, would join the others and sit down formally and courteously. The women, on the other hand, whether at the entrance itself or in the courtyard, would slap their thighs with their hands and, wailing, would try to embrace the ice-covered corpse of Bhagwan Kaur. This would provoke the other women to start wailing again and one or two would try to stop the newcomer from falling over the body. The more they were restrained, the greater efforts they made.

This had been going on since morning. The wailing women would stop once in a while to claim the most concern and affection.

"Oh Mother! Why didn't I also die along with you...."

"My dearest one, take me with you...."

"Oh most gracious one! Get up and speak to me just once more...."

Just then a woman came running towards us from the courtyard. She called out to Gurchetan's younger brother, Harmeet: "Son! Quickly. Run and fetch Lalchand. The youngest daughter-in-law has fainted!"

Immediately, Harmeet took his scooter and went off to fetch the hakim Lalchand. And the woman returned to the courtyard.

"What time has been fixed for the cremation?" I asked Gurchetan in a whisper.

"We are still waiting for a few relatives. Harmeet's in-laws haven't come yet nor has the middle daughter reached. It won't be before half past one or two."

They were blessed with a large extended family. Bhagwan Kaur had three sons and three daughters, all married. The girls as well as the boys. All into prosperous homes. Some were officers in the police or in the army. The various in-laws and their relations were expected to come in full force and with proper respect. It doesn't matter about the others but they must definitely await the parents of the daughters-in-law as well as all the relatives from the homes into which the daughters were married or else they would hear of it for the rest of their lives.

"It is best to wait for them," an older man was telling the others even though he was really uncomfortable with the increasing heat. "Relations with in-laws are lifelong, but they are as delicate as the threads on a loom. If they get tangled, they have to be broken before a new knot is tied. The relationship always remains. Don't worry. They'll arrive in a while. It is worth waiting. On such occasions one has to be specially careful. During weddings such things can be glossed over. Nor is it easy to come away at such short notice. A hundred things need to be taken care of, a hundred things need to be done.

Gurchetan was the one I knew best. We had studied together up to the tenth and then he started farming. But we used to meet every two or three days to exchange formal greetings if nothing else. In any case I had never been a frequent visitor to his home. There had never been any need. As is the custom in the village, I acknowledged Bhagwan Kaur as my Tai, as my father's elder brother's wife – an older aunt – but I had actually spoken to her only twice or thrice.

Looking at Bhagwan Kaur it is difficult to imagine that she was seventy years old. She was a tall woman. Robust but not plump, fair and with large eyes. There was not a single wrinkle on her face. She wore heavy gold ear rings and a pendant around her neck, and gold bangles. Gurchetan's father, Bohad Singh, was no match for her. A few inches shorter, dark, with eyes sunken and small, he was quite unprepossessing. His beard was scanty, and, in the last few years, he had developed a big belly. However, he was among the well-to-do respected persons in the village. I used to wonder how Bhagwan Kaur's parents had chosen him for her. In no respect did he seem suitable as a match for her. Yes, sometimes I also used to think that perhaps the attraction was the prospect of what he would inherit. He was the only son of a landed farmer. There was no sister, no brother. Without any other family obligations, the entire heap of wealth fell into his lap. Under such circumstances, who would ever ask the preference of the girl? When someone buys a cow and pulls on the rope does he ever give a thought to what the cow might be feeling....? It will look back repeatedly. Its eyes full of tears and it will low. But the new owner will merely tug firmly on the rope and drag it away. Who knows the same thing might have happened to Bhagwan Kaur!

Well. However it came about now she was an important and well-placed leader in the community. Gurchetan and two of the daughters had taken after her, with the same kind of build and colour, tall and strapping. The other children looked like Bohad Singh. Those who didn't know the family usually thought that the children belonged to two different families.

Suddenly, another bout of loud crying roused me from my reverie. A Sumo vehicle had just stopped outside. Perhaps the middle daughter had arrived along with her father-in-law and mother-in-law and other relatives. Gurchetan promptly got up and took her in his arms. She continued to cry clinging to her brother for a while and then, wailing and keening she went inside to their mother's bier and sitting next to the charpai rocked back and forth, hitting her head on the wooden frame. The women sitting around, who had quietened down, once again broke out crying.

Just then my Bhua, Diya Kaur, got up and, wiping her eyes and walking slowly, beckoned me. When I reached her she said in a soft, tear-soaked voice, "Son, I can't walk. When you are ready, drop me at the cremation ground on your scooter."

She was a large, fat woman. Her knees were crippled with pain. She was a widow and had no children. She seldom went to her in-laws now. She lived mostly with her younger brother, my Chacha who ploughed the fields of her father-in-law, sowed the seeds, and collected the harvest. A few jealous people pointed fingers at him: "He is appropriating his sister's fields." But neither the sister nor the brother paid any attention to what people said.

Bhua was a close friend of Bhagwan Kaur. When Bhagwan Kaur fell ill, she visited her every day. Sometimes she would even hobble over by herself regardless of the pain. For the last two days she had stayed with her all the time. Gurchetan told me, "I don't know what they talked about. We could never understand their conversation. Sometimes they would laugh, and sometimes cry. One day they sat close together, singing."

"How did Bhua know that Tayi was ill?" I had asked him casually.

"The day she took a turn for the worse, Bebe had said, 'Send for Diya Kaur. I want to talk.' So we brought her. One day Bhua remarked: 'Son, I recognised your mother after thirty years!' We were quite surprised – we had never seen Bhua visiting Bebe, so how was this close friendship possible? After that, whenever she came to her maternal home Bhua would come to spend time with Mother. Sometimes they would talk till it became dark and she would then just stay over. It is only during the last two years that she started visiting...."

"The older people still retain ties of love and affection. These days even fathers and sons are at daggers drawn! Between daughters, daughters-in-law, and mothers too there is no love lost." An older man sitting behind me put in who obviously had been listening to Gurchetan.

I had to go to work and looked for a way to excuse myself. I asked Gurchetan very politely: "I expect the cremation won't be till at least one-thirty or two?"

"At least! Otherwise the relations will object that we didn't wait for them."

"Bhua can't walk. I'll drop her at the cremation ground. Do

you need anything done there?" I asked and got up.

"No. Thanks. What work can there be? The boys have already taken a cartload of wood and dung cakes."

"Right. I'll see you there then." I said as I took my leave with folded hands and went across to where Bhua was – she had been watching to see when I would leave.

"Shall we go, Son?" She said promptly as she struggled to get up, her hands on her knees pushing hard.

"If you wish. But if you want to stay, I'll come back for you."

"No, Son. There is no need to stay now. The women have started bathing Bhago.... If you need to go anywhere else, you carry on. I'll sit there and wait." She said and she started walking out.

By the time she reached the scooter outside she was breathing heavily and soaked in sweat.

"Oh dear! My body is giving up now. Bhago wasn't – Oh dear! – like this at all! Don't know what happened to the wretch! In a matter of minutes.... Son, I recognised her after thirty years! I asked her: 'Hey! Aren't you Miriam? Bashir's daughter?' She had replied in a studied way – 'Miriam died that same night, my friend, the night when I saw my father, my mother, my brother and my sister being herded away, at dagger point, like cattle...'."

"Miriam....?" I stopped short – I was about to kick start the scooter – and my mouth fell open in astonishment.

"Yes, Son. She was the daughter of Bashir of Nava Pind. During the riots the Nihang, Tega Singh, abducted her."

I was absolutely stunned to hear this. None of my companions in the village had an inkling of this. All of us thought that Bhagwan Kaur was a Jat.

A hundred questions surfaced in my mind. If she was Bashir's daughter, how did she come to be with Bohad Singh? How did they get married? Why didn't Miriam's father and mother look for her? Why didn't anyone object to the match? Afterwards, during the scrutiny of those who were left behind, why did Miriam conceal her identity?

The mid-day sun was raining fire. Seeing me standing there dumbfounded, Bhua asked, worried: "If it is too hot for you, don't worry about me. I'll get there myself."

"No, no. Bhua. Sit," I said as I started the scooter. I was sure that Bhua knew much more.

We reached the cremation ground taking the route by the big pond at Phirni. I stopped under the dappled shade of a tree. The cart with the wood and the dung cakes had already reached. Two men were unloading the wood and placing it near the platform where the corpses are burnt.

"Son, can you get me some water to drink?" Bhua asked as she looked for a shady place to sit, running her tongue over her lips and mopping the perspiration from her face with one end of her dupatta.

I looked around for water. To one side there was a tap but there was no vessel next to it. I asked the cart driver. He had a tin mug.

As I handed Bhua the mug of water I looked around. In that

scorching noon heat, the cremation ground itself seemed to be on fire. The tin roof over the place for the pyre was black with soot. On one side there was a scrawny keekar tree which had a nest on top – perhaps of an eagle or a crow – but there were no birds to be seen. The platform under the tree, built by the panchayat, was covered with dry bird droppings and the area around it was covered with feathers and dried twigs. Occasionally, when the wind rose, it would whip up the ashes from a recently burned pyre which would then slowly settle over the area covering the trees and all other vegetation, people and the earth itself.

Bhua cleared a little space on the platform and sat down. The questions in my mind pricked like fish bones. To continue the conversation, I asked innocuously: "Bhua, we have always considered Bhagwan Kaur to be the daughter of Jat Sikhs."

"Not at all. She was Bashir's daughter. Bashir Randhawa's." She replied confidently.

"Then.... Bhagwan Kaur... Bohad Taya...?" Bhua understood my confusion, and my curiosity, and continued.

"It was then, you know, at the time you got Independence, during all those killings and stabbings....Tega from our village abducted her from Nava Pind. He dragged her into the fields... she was so beautiful. She must have been about ten or eleven then...."

With rapt attention I began to listen to my aunt narrate her first hand experience of those black pages of our history. I was careful not to interrupt her or to ask any questions for fear of breaking her train of thought. Bhua sat there, with eyes half closed, face to face with those terrible happenings in her past.

"Tega, Son, was about to kill the girl. He had drawn his krpan from its scabbard. Just then Tehal Singh, Bohad's father, reached the spot. He called out: 'Fool! Why are you committing this heinous sin? Just look at the girl! How will you ever expiate the sin of killing this poor innocent girl? Hand her over to me. I'll take her home. I'll take her to the gurudwara, give her amrit and bring her up in the faith as my own daughter. I don't have a daughter of my own, I have only one son, Bohad. The brother and sister can grown up together.'

"They say, Son, that Tega did not agree at first. He insisted that she was the offspring of the Turks and that he would despatch her to their Heaven. The girl's screams and shrieks were heartrending and Tehal Singh could not bear them. He offered money – a princely sum – 'Here! I'll give you six times twenty rupees! Give the girl to me.' Tega agreed and Tehal brought the girl home. On the auspicious day of sangrand, he gave her amrit at the gurudwara and so Bhagwan Kaur was born. He frightened her by telling her that if she stepped out of the house Tega Singh would get her. And that if she tried to escape he himself would kill her. They say that the girl was so terrified that she never even crossed the threshold of the inner rooms.... I, too, couldn't have been more than eleven or twelve then. Occasionally my mother would take me to Tehal Chacha's house, it was all part of the larger family. I became very attached to Miriam. We would be together inside the whole day, we would embroider sheets or spin on the charkha. Even though her name was now

Bhagwan Kaur I always called her Miriam. Once Tehal Chacha scolded me but she took me inside and begged me: 'You must always call me Miriam!'"

Bhua paused awhile. Though I too had seen that dark period I had understood very little then of what all had been going on. Why there was so much smoke coming from people's homes. Why people clung to each other crying. I can understand it all now – what must have gone on and how it had affected the minds of both lots of people. I can even feel it now. And I know even this – if death does not strike then somehow all such atrocities lose their horrifying image.

Bhua continued. "I would ask Miriam softly, 'Where could your abba be? Your ammi, your older sister Fatima, your younger brother Feroze, your aunt Noor?' She would put her hand on my mouth, and her eyes full of tears, she would say: 'No. No… Tega will kill me or Bohad's father will.' And she would sob. She never wept aloud…. Gradually she started calling Tehal Singh 'Bapu'. And she became fond of the cows and buffaloes. She named one of the cows Fatima. And she called one of the buffalo calves Feroze. She loved to call them and would spend the whole day talking to them. Sometimes she would say, 'You are my ammi,' or 'You are my aapa'…" Bhua sighed deeply. Then she drank some water from the tin mug and asked me, "Take a look, Son. Are they coming or not with Bhago?"

I looked across the pond, into the far distance towards the village. "No, Bhua. I can't see them anywhere." I was still very curious about Miriam and I asked, "Then how did she get married to Bohad Taya if she was considered to be his sister?"

"Who knows, Son, how everything happened. Within three years she had gained so much height that she had to stoop to step over the threshold. And what beauty! Tehal Singh began to get very worried. The boys in the village knew. They were getting ideas and thinking...She is a Muslim after all! What could Tehal Singh do to them? But Tehal Singh was a wise man. He took her to his own mother-in-law's house and left her there. Then I got married and for the next thirty years we didn't meet..." And Bhua sighed heavily again.

I said nothing. Looking down I scraped away the bird droppings on the platform. Then Bhua herself continued: "I got to know afterwards, when we met. She herself told me.... Tehal Singh's mother-in-law was old. The young men there, too, started getting interested, and would peer over the wall. She sent a message: 'Take Bhago away.' They say that Tehal Singh consulted with the village elders. Overnight he brought the girl back from his in-laws' and the very next morning solemnised her marriage with Bohad in the gurudwara.

"Didn't Miriam demur or object?" I asked Bhua feeling sad myself.

"She, whose spirit had been deadened, why would she object, Son? First she was taken into the faith as a daughter, and now she became a daughter-in-law within the same faith. You know what Bohad looks like – he'd already been rejected by four different families! Perhaps Tehal Singh felt that his chances of finding a bride were slim. Moreover, where would he ever find one as beautiful as this?

And there was no expenditure involved. It would also put an

end to speculation and gossip. But this true-begotten daughter showed exemplary qualities throughout her life and God showered good luck and prosperity on her. Within a few years she bore three sons and three daughters. Fortune and happiness filled her house. And people soon forgot about the past. Her sons turned out to be honourable. Her daughters were married into affluent families – they all have plenty. Tractors, Maruti cars, scooters, but you know all about that. But I was totally unaware of it all because I never came to my parent's home. I wanted to come back only after your uncle died. What would I have come for before? I was sure that Miriam must be long dead and gone. But, one day, I recognised her in the gurudwara! I asked her, and she replied, 'Miriam died long ago. I am Bhagwan Kaur.' I couldn't stop staring at her...."

Bhua guffawed sarcastically and then continued as though talking to herself. "Hunh! She said Miriam is dead! And, I am Bhawan Kaur...! Yes, I could see the black thread on her shoulder of the kirpan which she wore under her clothes. Then she took me aside and asked me, 'Aren't you Diya Kaur?' Well, after that we used to meet every day. She told me that her eldest son was the sarpanch of the village. One son was a lawyer at the courts, and the last a teacher. She told me that one daughter was married to the thanedar, the second one's husband was in the army. The youngest daughter had mirgrated to Canada. 'You see, Miriam died a long time ago. Now I am Bhagwan Kaur, the Jathedarni!' ...You know, Son, she would laugh and joke with me unreservedly. But I know how women think and feel. I knew that in her heart there was no laughter. I wanted to ask her: 'Do you not think of your abba and ammi?' But I was too scared to ask.... Now you see, Son. Jathedarni Bhagwan Kaur too has gone..." Bhua took a deep breath, and then asked me: "Look, Son. Are they bringing her?"

Far away, at the turning just outside the village, I could see a crowd of people with the bier. "They are still far, Bhua," I told her.

Strange thoughts started churning in my mind. Where would her parents be? Were they dead or alive? Who knows they might have been murdered while they were on their way in one of the refugee convoys! Even if they were alive, how would they possibly know that the daughter they thought was dead was in fact leaving behind such a large well-placed family.

"Son! Shall I tell you something else?" Bhua said suddenly. "The day Bhago lost consciousness, I was with her. She was burning hot, running a high fever. The doctor had said she should have an ice compress on her forehead. I was doing that as she lay there with her eyes closed, almost lifeless. Then she started muttering, loudly. 'Abba! Abba! A... The bear has caught me! The bears are dragging me away...Abba... Where are you? Oh! Fatima! I've fallen into a well.... I'm drowning.... I don't want to go into that thicket.... The brute's taking me there.... I'll be scratched and pricked.... Oh! Feroze! Stop the brute....! Abba... Come! ...Abba...Ammi... Fatima...Come! Oh! Feroze....! Oh! Nobody hears me!...I keep crying, calling out.... Where is everybody...?" And then she fainted.

"We were all shocked. Her family was shocked. Whatever had happened to Bhagwan Kaur? She remembered none of her sons, nor any of her daughters.... Who was she calling out to? All her life she had looked after such a large household and family ... but when she lost consciousness where did her mind revert...?"

Bhua sat there, still stupefied. Such things were beyond her comprehension.

"Bhua, did Tayi speak again?" I asked.

"She did, Son." Bhua said looking extremely sad. "She regained consciousness for a little while. ...The poor woman kept crying out as before... Then she hiccupped a few times and – that's it."

Bhua fell silent. She wiped the tears from her eyes.

I saw that people had reached the gates of the cremation ground with the bier of Jathedarni Bhagwan Kaur.

NOVEMBER 1984

Ajeet Cour

Those were black days, bloody days, full of a strange fear of death. A choking sensation rose from the earth to the sky, like a black cloth smothering all.

It was the month of November. The beginning of the month. The year was 1984. The city had been in shock, stunned, since 31 October. The woman who had ruled the country for so many years, the woman who had launched an attack on Harimandir Sahib at Amritsar like Abdali, the woman who had treated the country as her private property, that most exalted empress had been assassinated.

Of course assassination is deplorable. Reprehensible. But in this country it has not been uncommon for kings or queens to be assassinated. Here a king imprisoned his own father, murdered him, chopped up his brothers, and then proceeded to rule the country. This country also saw the assassination of the man who

---

November chaurasi. Translated by Satjit Wadva

was popularly known as the Father of the Nation, a secular nation. But after any such assassinations, death did not hover over the defenceless and innocent citizens of the nation.

This time, people were being killed openly, out in the streets. Herds of people, instigated and guided by their leaders, roamed the streets and bylanes of the city, causing mayhem. Homes were looted, burnt. People slaughtered.

This too has happened before. Exactly like this. When the father of this empress had agreed that this country be partitioned, cut into two, and that too with a blunt knife. Then too a savage madness had the people in its grip. Then too homes had been set afire, like now. Then, too, people had knives driven into their abdomens. They were disembowelled; and their guts pulled out in bunches were scattered on the naked roads, in the fields, and on footpaths.

Then, too, fear, like a vulture, had hovered and circled over the cities and the villages.

Today, thirty-seven years later, the same thing is happening again.

I had closed all the doors and windows of the house and sat inside with my daughter, Arpana, on 31 October, and the first three days of November.

Our neighbours destroyed the name plate hanging on the gate downstairs. They telephoned to reassure us: "Don't worry. We are here to protect you."

But when thousands were being murdered in the colonies

across the Jamuna, it was not possible to remain locked up, like cowards, in the house.

It had been announced on the TV and on the radio that the military had taken charge of the law and order situation in the city. But if the military was guarding the city, how would we able to leave the house? We would have to cross the bridge over the river to get there. Surely we will be stopped. They will ask what business we have there....

We would try. We would see how far we get. We could not remain holed up, cowering inside, while people were being killed on the streets, their heads bashed with iron rods, drenched in petrol and set on fire alive. Or being burnt with kerosene-filled rubber tubes around their necks, their homes torched. Or when women were being smoked out of burning homes and sexually assaulted right there, next to the bodies of their sons or husbands. Right there on the naked streets, covered with blood and mud, these atrocities were being committed. Entire crowded bastis were being devastated. Already in the grip of death and poverty there was no recourse for them. In the midst of this murderous outrage, to think only of our own safety was not possible.

On the TV and the radio there was a constant replay of the last words of the slain empress: "...Every drop of my blood.... Bood! Blood! Blood...!"

We, my daughter Aparna and I, set out from the house. The driver was a Hindu and I felt that the fact of his being a Hindu would be a protective shield for us.

That year the winter seemed to have set in early. We decided to take some food with us – packets of tea, sacks of sugar, milk powder, and some blankets. We turned towards Azad market to get the blankets because that is where the thick army blankets are available.

As we were about to turn in to Paharganj from Chitragupt Road, right in front of the Paharganj police station, we saw a mob shouting in frenzy. The slogan they were raising was: "Khoon ka badla khoon!" - Blood will be avenged with blood!

As our car crawled past this crowd, I felt choked as though a lump of ice was stuck in my throat. This is terror! A primeval fear! The fear of death… a numbing fear that my daughter, sitting beside me, could be dragged out by the hooligans….

Having got the blankets, we crossed the bridge across the Jamuna. We saw no soldiers, nor any police. There was no official there. Nor could we see any turbans. There was no Sikh out on the road.

Proceeding slowly, we reached the Gandhi Nagar school. A police truck was parked outside the gate and there were two or three policemen relaxing in it, drinking tea.

Inside the gate there was a flood of humanity. So many people! All in the school building, so tightly packed that a needle couldn't have got through. Terrified, they stood in stunned silence. They were crowded filling all corners, crammed into that space with their backs to the walls. Women, children, men, and old people.

It seems someone deep in the crowd recognised me. He raised both his arms, and in a tearful trembling voice said with a heartrending sigh: "Bibiji! Not tanks of blood! Now there are wells filled with blood."

Perhaps he had read my article after the attack on the Golden Temple – "Tanks of Blood".

Hardly five months had passed since then. And now....

There was no room for the car, but they insisted: "Bring the car inside, just inside the gate. Who knows what will happen outside? Someone will set it on fire...."

They squashed closer together, everyone shrinking back perhaps an inch till there was enough space for the car. What amazing people! They had lost everything themselves and yet they were concerned for my car.

We unloaded the car. They said: "There is no need. The langar is working, we have enough to eat. You shouldn't have taken the trouble...."

Behind the school building, in what used to be the playground, there were large chulas burning. On one dal was simmering, and on the other rotis were being made.

"But how do all these provisions get here?"

"Oh! There is one Kishenlal ji. Morning and evening he brings sacks full of dal and atta. All the shops are closed. But they say he begs or borrows, or just breaks open locks on shops and brings the stuff. We have to survive somehow... and there must easily be ten or fifteen thousand people here! Kishenlal ji has taken it upon himself to see that we have enough food."

Human beings were being slaughtered, but humanity still survived.

In the playing field at the back some fifteen or twenty badly wounded persons were lying on the bare earth. Only one person had something under him – his wife's dupatta. She herself, her head uncovered, sat huddled next to him, hugging her knees to her chest, weeping.

In the morning these people had been taken to a hospital in the police truck but the hospital authorities had refused to admit them saying, "Those people will burn our hospital down." 'Those people,' meaning the attacking mobs.

There were some with severe burns on their legs and arms. Others had their heads crushed, and yet others had broken limbs. It was a terrifying sight. There was a strange helplessness. A shocked fear. An abject resignation.

We came back to Connaught Place. Bought bottles of Dettol, bandages, tubes of antiseptic creams and returned to do whatever we could to clean and dress their wounds.

And then, for the first time, I felt a revolting stench in the air as the wind had changed direction. Obviously all these people, having been cooped up like so many chickens in a basket for so many days, had to relieve themselves somewhere. The building was enclosed from all sides apart from the gate which was open, but no one had the courage to go out.

This was a ghetto! This is how those Jews must have lived, those who were able to flee from the atrocities of the Nazis and take refuge collectively in a derelict town in Poland. Terrified of death, they had sought shelter in underground sewage pipes, or in man-hole tunnels, or in deserted attics.

When it became dark, we left that place to drive straight to Khushwant Singh's house. It was 9.30 p.m. No relative or friend is allowed in Khushwant Singh's house at this time. His home is closed for visitors at 9 o'clock.

But this was a day of doom. This day all rules and laws had broken down.

Khushwant opened the door.

I don't cry in anyone's presence. But that night...the shock of the whole day, the helplessness, the fear, the horror, they all poured out of my eyes with my tears. With my head resting on his shoulders I sobbed loudly, helplessly, and Arpana silently wiped her eyes with her dupatta.

I told Khushwant everything. He listened in stunned silence, and absolute amazement. I suggested to him: "Next to the Gandhi Nagar School building is the building of Shyam Lal College. All schools and colleges are closed. If you can speak to the Lieutenant Governor and ask him to open the College premises then these thousands of people will get some space to sit, or even stretch out."

Khushwant said he had been trying to reach the Governor for three or four days. But these days, whether it is a minister, a police officer or any government official including the Governor, there was a standard response: "Sahib is not available."

These days no one was anywhere. No one seemed to exist.

And that was the truth. The whole country was wrapped in the eye of a whirlwind. It was not dust that the wind whipped up, but blood. The sun had vanished. And the sky itself was hiding behind a bloody veil.

"I'll try again," Khushwant said. "I'll phone again at night. I'll call his residence. Is anything worse possible than what has already happened? And what do I have to lose? For two days I took refuge at the Swedish embassy, with my entire family... We returned home today because the government announced that the city has been put under army rule and nothing will happen now...."

"The army? We didn't see any signs of the military the whole day! Hardly a furlong away from the Gandhi Nagar school a mob killed twelve people! And something must have happened in Paharganj too because a bloodthirsty mob had collected there. We passed by there. We crossed the Jamuna bridge four times....and there was no military anywhere. Take care of yourselves! Keep the doors shut."

It was about 2.30 that night when it occurred to me that an extremely good doctor at the Medical Institute – Harbans Singh Wazir – was the personal physician to the President of India, Giani Zail Singh. It doesn't matter how blinded a person can be because of his rank and position, or how weak, he cannot ignore his doctor. So I called Dr Wazir. "Please tell Giani ji to at least get Shyam Lal College opened for these refugees. And, Harbans, if possible please ask him to get fifteen or twenty temporary lavatories done. And the same number of sweepers.... Let them at least dig pits in the ground. There is a real risk of cholera breaking out. Can you send an ambulance there? Some people are wounded. Just lying there in the dust with open wounds...They could get gangrene, and certainly turn septic."

I don't know whether it was because of Harbans' efforts or Khushwant's influence but on the third day the rooms of Shyam Lal College were opened, temporary lavatories were made and the sweepers also came.

For the wounded Harbans sent not only an ambulance but also a team of doctors.

Some artists, social workers, and theatre people came together to form a group. They would meet early in the morning in Lajpat Bhawan which was a central collecting point for food, clothes, shoes, blankets and quilts. They would sort them and send out vans with the provisions to different camps in the city.

Aparna and I also joined them. The group worked systematically and the service and help they rendered was therefore more effective.

None of these people were sentimental or emotional. They were motivated by a deep sympathy for their fellow human beings. They didn't weep or cry like me. They were like soldiers in battle. Leaving the comfort of their homes, away from their loved ones, they were committed to the common cause of safeguarding humanity from the onslaught of barbarous high-handed hooliganism.

The gates of Shyam Lal College were opened. The rooms were also unlocked. But no one was willing to go, to leave the safe haven of the school and step out onto the narrow street between the school and the college. To step out onto that street was to step into the kingdom of death! To go out on the street meant that they would be at the mercy of the murderous mobs. To be out on a street was to invite danger, to walk into a seething cauldron of trouble.

What a strange age! When man should be petrified to go out!

"Let's break down the back wall of the Gandhi Nagar school, and make a corresponding opening in the back wall of the college so that people don't have to cross the road." I suggested.

"But the police...?"

There were two policemen sitting on the raised platform under a tree in the back yard of the school. I took them aside and spoke to them. "We have to do this.... How much money will you want?"

They hesitated ever so slightly. They didn't speak for about five seconds but kept looking at each other. "But what if the school and college authorities object later...?"

"Don't worry about that. It is my responsibility to have both the walls repaired."

I paid them. Then they said, "What if you don't get them fixed?"

I showed them my press card and also gave each one my visiting card.

"Do me a favour. The police truck that is parked at the gate, please park it at the head of the street. We will close the gates of both buildings. Should any attackers come, they will have to come from the lane and you will be standing there. Then there won't be any danger."

I knew very well that in those days the biggest danger was from the police itself because every bloodthirsty mob was accompanied by a protective unit of police. It was in such police jeeps that jerrycans of petrol and kerosene were carried to those settlements where the mobs set people on fire and burnt down homes. Policemen too were among those who looted and raped.

In fact in some places the police had gone in first and collected all arms – mostly kirpans and sticks and occasionally a revolver or gun. They said that it was in the interest of keeping peace. When the people had thus been disarmed, the screaming mobs came.... The massacres were done in the style of Ghengis Khan or Timur within the knowledge of the police and with their blessings. But what blessings? They said these were the orders they had received. But then in this country there is always a reward for any favour done. From the constable to the minister, from the peon to the Prime Minister, everyone dispenses favours to those in need, and collects the fees due. Showering favours every moment. And grateful thanks are given for every such consideration!

These attacks were different from the attacks of earlier times – whether Ghengis Khan, Timur or Nadir Shah. Those people were fired with laudable ambitions – they were conquering kingdoms, expanding empires, extending their territories – even though they, in the pursuit of glory and victory, marched through rivers of blood. These attacks merely displayed a poverty of ideals and were proof of their own basest beastliness.

In the depths of my being I felt memories being revived; these attacks, these murders, were like those committed by the Nazis, methodically and in cold blood. Armed with lists of names, they used to ferret out the Jews. But perhaps they were not so cruel as to pull out people – men, women, children who hid like mice –

from gutters and manholes, and then separate them on the basis of their usefulness. And then send them to concentration camps and gas chambers accordingly. It was only one man, Hitler, who was cruel. The others were merely obeying orders. Some in a more cruel manner, others in a less callous way.

Six million Jews were murdered.

And today, when I write after nine years and three months of the blood bath of November 1984, hundreds of thousands of people are being killed in Bosnia, Sarajevo and Rwanda. It has been going on for two years.

And in my own country, the blood bathed pages of Bhiwandi, Malyana and Mumbai flutter before my eyes, the pages of which history will always be ashamed. And in Punjab and Kashmir, and Assam and Bihar – everywhere it is overcast with dark red clouds of blood. And the fearsome memory of Nagasaki and Hiroshima still makes our hair stand on end.

Man! The supreme creation of God! In whose heart the barbaric animal is still alive, screaming for blood!

Anyway, the walls of the school and College buildings were broken to give those people a little bit more space. Even so, there were still about fifteen families in each room. They spilled over into the verandah too, and into the open compounds as well.

For almost a month, we – Arpana and I – stayed there from morning till midnight.

On the seventh day, Mother Teresa's missionaries brought tins of milk powder and biscuits for the women and children.

They spent the entire day, day after day, feeding the hungry children and tending the sick.

On the tenth day a tent was pitched. And a small, fat man, an officer of the government, occupied it. Half a dozen policemen hovered around him day and night.

The first thing he did was to put a lock on our store room. The room in which we put the things we ourselves had bought, or collected from friends, relatives, and neighbours. Things like blankets and quilts, stocks of food and medicines.

We got to know of it at nine at night, the time that we would go from room to room and distribute blankets and quilts as required. It was done very systematically. First lists were made. Then blankets collected from the store would be distributed. Groups of workers were in charge of separate wings. Each of them was responsible for taking care of the refugees in his wing.

When the lists were ready we went to the store to find it locked, and an armed policeman guarding it.

"Who has locked this?" I asked in some surprise.

"Sahib has." The Sahib's agent said arrogantly.

"Sahib? What Sahib?"

"He joined duty today. He is a government Sahib." He offered casually.

"Where is he?"

"Find out from his office."

"Where's the office?"

"There, in the tent."

In the tent another couple of armed policemen were relaxing, their legs stretched out resting on a tabletop, as though they had come to a wedding party.

"Where is Sahib?"

"He must be somewhere here!" They replied nonchalantly as though to say, "Get lost!"

"Here, where?" I was beginning to get angry, and a little bold too because some of our people had also reached. They whispered in my ear, "Be careful! These sons of bitches can be nasty….they could also throw us out. Those who get people killed, can do anything!"

"All they can do is kill. So, a few more will get killed!" I was furious. I ranted: "Tell us where he is! He is not in the camp… we have just been around it."

"Then he must have gone for dinner. It's dinnertime. He has to eat, doesn't he?" one of them snapped back.

We waited for two hours for him to return. When he came, he was chewing paan and reeking of liquor.

"Are you the in-charge? The new in-charge?"

"Yes. I am!" he thundered at us.

"And where were you till eleven o'clock?"

"I'm not answerable to you," he replied in English.

"No. You aren't answerable to anyone! You are the Government. The Government is…."

"What do you want?" he snarled.

"Why have you had the store locked?"

"Why shouldn't I lock it? I am in charge of this camp."

"That's obvious. With all the security you have for yourself! You must be a senior officer. Have you inspected the camp? Have you done any good to anyone? Have you registered a single complaint, a report? Have you appointed anyone to trace the missing members of any family? Nothing! All you have done is to lock the store.... And you have come after TWO hours, chewing paan...!"

"I'll have you arrested for insulting a Government officer...."

"Yes. Why not? You can arrest me, you can get me liquidated – in jail or outside! I am fully aware of your power. You can do what you want, but right now unlock the store."

"The store will NOT be opened!"

"The store will definitely be opened, and NOW!" I retorted and produced my trump card – my Press Card. "Here! You can note down my name and address. Arrest me whenever you want. But first open that lock – not even a pin there belongs to the Government. Everything in it has been bought by our own money, money earned by our efforts, not bribe money!"

He looked a bit shaken as all this went on in front of his subordinates. He had the lock opened, but said softly, "I'll see to you later!" It didn't seem to be a threat but merely embarrassment.

In this camp there were ten to fifteen thousand people who had ten to fifteen thousand stories to tell. And there were as many stories from the camps at Trilokpuri, Uttam Nagar, Shahdara and their adjoining colonies. I will tell you only three of them.

One woman sat in the corner of one room, her four children huddled around her. Whenever we urged her to go to the langar for her meals she would simply shake her head. "Food for the children? Milk?" The response was the same dejected "No".

One day passed. Two days. Three days went by.

By that time she was no longer sitting. She had sunk to the floor, lifelessly, helplessly. Her children clung to her legs and belly, digging their knees into their stomachs, their heads drooping.

"She doesn't eat herself, nor does she allow her children to eat. What should we do?"

We brought in people from other rooms to find out if anyone knew her. Perhaps someone from her own colony would recognise her. At last we found one man, who went and sat next to her and talked to her: "Bibi, get up. Have courage. You are not the only victim... everyone has been hurt." The woman opened her eyes a little, and then started crying uncontrollably, helplessly.

"Let her cry. If she cries, only then will she be able to see her children. If she cries, only then will she think of feeding them."

Then that man told us that on the night of 2 November the mobs attacked her colony.

'They had dragged her husband out into the street, hit him with iron rods and then put petrol on him and burnt him. Her eldest son remained inside hiding behind a big tin trunk. She took the other children and ran out into the street.... The neighbours pulled her and her children into their home and hid them.

'The mob then set fire to her house. She was frantic and tried to open the door again and again. "Where is my Sohan? Let me go! Let me go and get him…they'll butcher him…."

'When the mobs departed shouting in victory and mad with glee, then the neighbours brought all of us, including this woman and her children, to this camp….

'She had gone in the middle of the night to her house looking for Sohan, her son. There was still smoke coming from the house which looked like a gaping hole, burnt to ashes.

'In the compound she had found Sohan's half burnt body. She thought that the dogs would find it and eat it. So she spent the rest of the night pulling down the remains of doors and windows and tried to burn the corpse of her son.

'We heard of this later when our neighbours told us she had gone to them to borrow kerosene oil and matches.'

This poor woman who pulled down bits of half burnt wood to cremate the body of her half burnt son! What else can happen to her?

The woman continued to sob uncontrollably. We brought water for her. She drank it. We put a plate of food before her. She broke a morsel with her trembling fingers and put it in her mouth….

I'll tell you the second story.

In the verandah there was an imposing man and his family. Next to him was his pretty plump and impressive wife, and a young son whose hair was cut like grass. It is the Sardarni's story.

'The factory was burnt. The house was robbed and then burnt. The neighbours hid us. When they brought us to the camp they begged me: "Bibiji, save your son's life! Cut his hair." So I cut his hair with these, my cursed hands…'

She wept bitterly.

Then wiping her tears with her dupatta she continued.

'The factory and the house don't matter. The Guru bestowed them, and he has taken them back. He knows best… He will look after us. He will grant them again. But Kaka's hair! Hai! How I used to take care of it! Washing it with curd… so beautiful, so thick, so silky. Such lovely golden brown hair!'

The third story is about a very old man who sat in one corner of the verandah. He had sat there for almost a week. Sometimes he would doze off leaning against the wall, his mouth slightly open, his white beard quivering as he shivered with the cold. His eyebrows were shaggy and white. He was wearing an old kurta pyjama and his head was bare.

We tried talking to him but he kept his eyes closed. At times though we could hear a soft murmur, 'Wahe Guru. Wahe Guru.' And he would sigh.

We found out that both his sons were auto rickshaw drivers. They didn't come home for two days. When his colony was attacked, he brought both his daughters-in-law and their children to the camp somehow – hiding and running to evade the attackers.

After two days the daughters-in-law left, saying they were

going to look for their husbands.

"And the children?"

"I don't know whether they've taken them along, or left them with somebody. How to find them in such a crowd...?" And his voice faltered.

At that moment I thought of Darji, my father. If he were alive he too might be sitting in a corner, just like this. His white beard would be trembling just like this old man's. I thanked God that he had passed on before he could see all this.

"Bapuji!" I touched him gently, "Please take this blanket. It is cold."

"No. Give it to a needy person."

"But what if you catch cold and get fever?"

"It will be good. I have nothing to live for."

I left the blanket next to him anyway. The next day it was exactly where I had put it. We tried our best but he would accept nothing, neither clothes nor the blanket.

On the seventh or eighth day I took a white turban for him. For a minute he looked at it. Then he looked at me. I don't know what it was about that look but I felt a searing heat. Even now sometimes at night I feel it shooting through me.

He accepted the turban with trembling hands. Slowly he unfolded it and, crumpling the width of it with both hands, started tying it, one fold after another.

When he had finished he looked at me again. Two tears spilled over from his eyes. They trickled down the creases in his cheeks leaving a trail of wetness and disappeared into his beard.

SPLINTERED

Raj Gill

A deserted road. Desolation all around. Not one person, or a trace of habitation. Not even a jackal or a fox. Far away perhaps some signs of living beings. Not a house. A room. Not much. Just a small eating shack and a kind of shed.

At least I'll be able to find out where I am. Mother must be worried, waiting. I've told her time and again not to stay up for me. Cover the food and leave it for me. You go to sleep. But the old woman will not listen! "I do so much for others and for my son I can't stay up a few hours?"

"But, Mother..."

"There's no need for any buts. When I get a daughter-in-law, I'll happily go to sleep!" The talk of marriage made me uncomfortable. To hell with such talk. Let's solve my current predicament! How am I to reach home? How am I to get out of

---

Tredhaan. Translated by Jasjit Mansingh

this wilderness? Would anyone believe that Delhi, which is bursting with glamour and gaiety, can also be flanked by such a dense wasteland!

Such were the thoughts of the man standing there. He was standing in the middle of the road like a rustic simpleton. But he didn't appear to be a fool, nor an illiterate villager. His imported clothes – a bush shirt from Manila, synthetic crease-free trousers from America and well made Chinese shoes – indicated that he was a gentleman from a prosperous family. The books he was holding in his hands revealed that he was educated. He was well built and handsome besides looking smart. But at that moment his face was clouded with fear, anger and apprehension.

No more drinking for me! Enough! Never again! If ever I drink, I won't eat anything! Ma! It makes me so sleepy. It is the third time it has happened.... He was thoroughly irritated with himself. In fact he was furious. He had spent the previous evening with his friend Kulbir and they had started drinking. Then they had gorged on generous helpings of saag and makki-di-roti. After dinner he had caught a bus from the market. It was the last bus. He had intended to get off at the main bus stop and take a taxi or scooter home. But he had dozed off in the bus and reached the Alipur bus depot. He got a great shock when the conductor informed him that the bus would go no further. After much pleading he was allowed to board the staff bus which was bound for Jahangirpuri. As soon as he leaned back in the seat he fell asleep again and instead of getting off at Azadpur, from where he could have taken a taxi, he reached the bus depot at

Jahangirpuri. This time the DTC staff let him off outside the depot. It was well past midnight. He had no idea where he was, nor would he have been any the wiser in the dark even if he did. Finally, he started walking towards the house he could see in the distance.

It was fortunate for him that it was an asphalt road or else he would have been stumbling through uneven fields. He began to get even more irritated as he walked. The sound of his footsteps reverberated like drumbeats. No matter how cautiously he trod, his footsteps could still be heard. All around him there was silence. For miles around it would be known that a man was walking there. He could be robbed! Let the bloody fools rob me! What will they get? My watch. About a hundred and fifty rupees. They are not likely to strip me of my trousers.

Suppose they do? Suppose they become greedy when they see expensive clothes? Oh God! Then instead of going home I'll have to go to the Jamuna. How can I go to the city stark naked. People will think I'm mad and they'll lock me up in a lunatic asylum! And I'll have to spend the rest of my life there.... Trembling, he stood stock still.

Should I just spend the night here on the side of the road? When day dawns surely I'll get a ride. Perhaps a bus, a tonga, or even a bullock cart. He was about to step off the road when he stopped, gripped by another fear. What if he should step on a snake or some other reptile! He imagined the worst. They didn't seem to be fields. It was wilderness. Where snakes lived! He started walking again. Towards that solitary house, quickening his pace. It was as though he wanted to outpace his own innermost thoughts.

When he reached the house he stopped. He didn't knock on the door. He thought instead of what kind of people lived there. Suppose they rob me and beat me to death. On the other hand, they might be terrified that I will go to the police and reveal their hideout. Surely in a house like this, out in the wilderness, there can be only bad characters! Like Kauda Rakshas – and it took Baba Nanak to come and reform him. For a moment he felt almost as though he was Nanak himself come to the door of this Kauda charged with the mission of rescuing him from his evil ways and setting him on the right path. Just then someone inside the house coughed and he instantly became Puran rather than Nanak and, frightened, backed away from the door. There was a pillar close by. He stood next to it, his legs and hands trembling. His feet ached, the city boots he was wearing were not suitable for tramping long distances. He leaned against the pillar, and within moments fell asleep.

In his sleep the books slipped out of his hands. The sound of them hitting the road was like the explosion of a firecracker. But he heard nothing. Nor was he conscious that the door behind him had opened. A man, a strong man who looked like a jat, emerged with a lathi in one hand and a lantern in the other. By the light of the lantern he first saw the books lying on the ground and then a man, leaning against the pillar, fast asleep. His heart filled with compassion. He touched the man to wake him up. The man woke with an agonised start and recoiled. His shoulder caught the pillar and he fell flat on his back. He looked up to see, towering over him as tall as a house, a man with a lathi. So, exactly what he had feared had happened, he thought trembling!

"Oh Brother. Get up. There is nothing to be frightened of," the jat reassured him. The tone was friendly. The words were spoken softly, calmly. He didn't seem to be a bad sort. Even so he got up cautiously. He smoothed his clothes brushing off the dust, picked up the books scattered on the ground, and stood before the man.

"The sound of your books falling woke me."

"I'm sorry. I dozed off."

"But at this time...," he stopped without finishing his sentence.

"I was in a bus. The bus brought me to this depot... I didn't know the way, I want to go to Delhi." He hesitated a while and then continued. "Can't I get a taxi hereabouts?"

"In this deserted place!"

"A bus?"

"At four o'clock in the morning."

The man looked at his watch. It was only two o'clock. Another two hours! What a terrible nuisance!

"But I must, I need to go."

"Nothing can be done just now. For the time being please come in and lie down. I'll wake you up at four o'clock to catch the bus."

"No. Really, please don't put yourself out. I'll wait here."

"Sir, what a thing to say! Do come in. …. We'll make you as comfortable as we can. Go in the morning."

Sure he will 'serve' me. Inside the house! So nobody outside can hear. Out here at least I'll scream and shout…somebody is bound to hear me. So thought the man but he said:

"No, Brother, it is quite all right here. Don't ruin your own sleep."

"There is no question of sleep if there is a traveller at my door."

"Well, I'll go and stand somewhere else," he retorted sharply.

"No. That wasn't the point. It is a matter of honour. Wretched is the man who cannot be hospitable and help a traveller who has lost his way.

"Listen. If you really want to be of some help, get me to Azadpur somehow or other."

The man thought for a while and then said, "Okay. Wait." He returned in a while wheeling his cycle.

"Let's go. It is quite far but never mind."

At Azadpur he didn't accept any money nor wait to be thanked. "If one man cannot help another, then who will."

Puran caught a taxi and reached his home in Kamala Nagar. He collapsed on his bed, with his boots on, and fell asleep.

"Ma!" He called out, irritated. It was half past five in the morning. He hadn't been given his cup of tea yet. She knows perfectly well that she should wake him up at five with a cup of tea.

"What is it, Son?"

"Where is the tea?"

"There is no milk."

"No milk? Why? Has the milk man dropped dead?"

"I don't know, Son. He hasn't come yet."

"Just let him come and see what he gets from me! We pay for it. It is not as though it is free. . . ."

The doorbell rang.

"At last he has come."

"Wait, Ma. I will talk to him."

Pulling on his gown he emerged from his room and went towards the door muttering to himself: First the wretched bus, then the wilderness. Now this milk man! All they want is money. Then, too, they can't bring it on time. We will get someone else who will be more punctual. It is not as though we have any obligation towards him....

He opened the door angrily. His mouth too fell open, as though his jaw had become unhinged.

Standing in front of him was the man he had met that night, the milk cans hung on the back of his cycle.

HE IS NOT THAT JASBIR

Prem Prakash

Hari Dev caught the last bus to town. As he settled in he turned around to look at the other passengers. He could see no Sikh with a black beard wearing either a dark blue or a saffron turban who could be feared as likely to hijack the bus.... All it needed was to thrust a revolver at the driver's neck and make him drive to a village where he and his terrorist companions would drag the Hindus out of the bus and shoot them.

There hadn't been any such incident for a long time but the fear of such brutality had become deeply etched in the hearts of people. Yet, anything can happen anytime. A bomb can explode in a bus, and turn it into a mortuary. Just the memory of such incidents in the past sent shivers up Hari Dev's spine.

As the bus started once again he turned to look at the passengers behind him. All the Sikhs were old. Right at the

---

Translated by Devinder Kaur Assa Singh and Jasjit Mansingh

back he saw one with lots of black in his beard but the way his turban was tied, and the kurta and pyjama he wore suggested he was just a villager. From his face and his expression he seemed to be a simple and innocent man.

Hari Dev relaxed and looked out of the window. He began thinking of the marriage of his friend's son which he had just attended. What a lot of money is spent on useless rituals! But only he spends who can afford it. Even so he must first have the desire to spend money. But even if he should not want to? Yes. Sometimes the desire itself can die even though it is desire alone that drives a man to act. Look at him for example. Despite the dangers of these troubled times he was travelling by bus.... All a person needs is a pistol. Rammed into the driver's neck, the bus is diverted. Then the victims are selected! The newspapers publish the details and photographs of the dead. Then people begin to comment: "He went to a wedding.... Who was to know only his corpse would return?" Death can happen anywhere. Even while sitting at home. Someone could knock on the door and call out.... Then, instead of delivering something, a message of congratulations, or even a gift, he opens fire – Bang! Bang! – then simply walks away.

Hari Dev's hand bumped against the window pane accidentally. He felt a piercing pain in the topmost joint of his little finger.... He turned around to look. That man with the black beard was looking at him! Hari Dev turned away and concentrated on the road ahead of the bus. There wasn't much traffic and the bus was going fast. ...You see the driver is a Hindu. He too is in a hurry to reach home before dark. It is also possible that he is a Jat Sikh after all. He could have cut his hair and trimmed his beard.... Once again, quite involuntarily, he looked back. That fellow was still looking at him! There were other Hindus in the bus, about ten, or eleven, or twelve.... Perhaps I am just imagining this. After all everybody has to look in front.... He resolved not to turn around and look back again.

When the bus stopped at the city terminal Hari Dev wanted to leave from the back of the platform. But that man was standing in a corner looking at him! To shake him off Hari Dev went to the gate that led to the car park. He saw the jeep of his friend the Excise Inspector, and he spoke to the driver who told him that he was supposed to receive an officer but he had not come. When Hari Dev got into the jeep the driver said he would first have to inform the officer's family, then he needed to buy vegetables for his own officer. Only then could he drive him home. Hari agreed to this circuitous route.

Half an hour later the jeep dropped him in the chowk. When he reached the turning into the lane where he lived he saw that same man standing in front of him. Hari Dev was not too nervous now. The man had no weapons in his hands and he himself was on home ground. However, sten guns can be carried under the armpit hidden in the folds of a shawl.... He began to walk past him suddenly frightened, and the man called out: "Hari! Have you not recognised me?"

Hari recognised the voice. It was his friend Master Jasbir Singh. He was dressed like a villager, and he had dyed his unkempt beard black to disguise himself. About a year or a year-and-a-half ago he had abandoned his home and his family to join the terrorists. It became known that he was alive when the government posted a reward of Rs 10,000 for information about him. The only news there had been of him till then was when he made contact once with a close friend at Amritsar. Hari Dev too had wanted to meet him. He even went to the village once to see how his children were faring. His family had wanted to leave the village to escape being harassed by the police. His wife had wept bitterly remembering the past. Hari Dev had wanted to give her some money but she had refused to take it, saying, "Virji, what shall I do with money...". Hari came from a nearby village and she quite naturally addressed him as Brother.

Hari shook hands with Jasbir but stopped short of an embrace. Earlier they did not shake hands but greeted each other affectionately with a bear hug.

"Let us go home," was all that Hari could say. Before he could knock, Jasbir cautioned him:

"Don't tell anyone at home that I am Jasbir.... We'll sit in the room upstairs."

As luck would have it, the door was not bolted and Jasbir went straight upstairs followed by Hari. He did not meet Hari's wife or sons and he ignored the dog Daboo who was wagging his tail, who also followed them.

Hari went downstairs to get some water and explained to his wife: "He is a class fellow... He has come from Khanna. You don't know him..."

By the time he took the water upstairs Jasbir had taken off

his turban and his shoes and was lying on the bed. His hair was mostly white.

"Will you have some tea?"

"Yes. And bring something to eat also, I'm very hungry."

While they were drinking tea, Hari noticed how much Jasbir had aged, and he appeared to be very weak. His eyes were sunken, and there were sagging pouches of flesh under his eyes. Where has he been? What has he been doing? How did his thinking change so suddenly? How could he have forgotten his progressive ideals? All these questions arose in Hari Dev's mind. The questions would begin to take shape in words and form sentences but then they would fight shy of emerging into the open. Finally he did ask a question: "Have you been keeping well?"

"No. I had malaria fever for ten days. There is no fever now but the weakness hasn't gone. And this wretched wound is not healing...," Hari said as rolled up his pyjama leg and bared his right leg. There was a dirty bandage on the wound.

"Take off this filthy bandage," Hari said and looked squarely at Jasbir. When Jasbir removed the bandage Hari saw that the wound was quite deep and long. Jasbir probed the skin in the area around the wound with his fingertips. He said, "Who knows... fucking gangrene may have set in."

"Shall we call Dr Loomba and let him examine it? Hari asked and Jasbir looked at him long and hard before shaking his head to indicate No. He feared that instead of the doctor the police may come.

"We can as well bandage it ourselves," Hari said and he went downstairs to fetch the dressings and medicine.

Finding Jasbir alone Daboo pawed his feet once or twice wanting to play. Then sitting on his haunches, he stretched his neck out, and looking pleadingly at Jasbir, barked a brief invitation. When he got no response, he sat again and wagged his tail. Then, still looking at him, he started to walk towards the head of the bed. Going down the stairs Hari began to fear that the police might actually come if they were hot on Jasbir's trail. Then he himself would get caught. He'd lose his job, and his family would starve.... Jasbir too used to say that starvation is worse than death.... He got a grip on himself, collected the medicines and took them upstairs. Then, just as a doctor would, he first cleaned the wound with spirit, applied the ointment in the gaping flesh, dusted antiseptic powder over it and bandaged it with a clean cloth. Cleaning his hands with a cotton wool swab and spirit, he asked, "How did you hurt yourself?"

"I was jumping over the wall and the prong blade of an upturned plough caught my leg." Hari listened and wondered how much truth there was in that statement.

"Had you gone somewhere on action?" At this direct question Jasbir looked again at Hari. Then, feeling shamefaced, he lowered his eyes. He said nothing. In the discussions they used to have earlier the word 'action' was part of their vocabulary during the height of the Naxalite movement, meaning specifically to exterminate, or in their case to reform a misguided classmate. Hari could not bring himself to use the word favoured by the Sikh terrorists for killing - 'sodhana' which also meant reform.

Jasbir had yet another euphemism – put them on a train.... But now they were meeting after two years. None of those words were appropriate at this meeting. To use them would be as blasphemous as using swear words in a place of worship.

"I had gone on no action," Jasbir was saying still looking down. "I was in somebody's house and the police raided it. I tried to run.... Then..."

"Let it be," Hari cut in. He knew that talking about the past would be painful and he wanted to avoid it. Thinking about it was bad enough. He changed the topic. "How are the children?"

"All right. I saw them at my wife's parents' home. I met your father's sister's husband Phuphad Girdhari too. He did not speak to me, just slunk away quietly."

"Has the older daughter's engagement been confirmed?"

"It is broken. The Doraha people went back on their word. Wasted Rs 7000 for nothing!"

Hari thought to himself, the terrorists loot so many banks and Jasbir is bemoaning the loss of Rs 7000? When I was giving his wife Rs 2000 she refused to take it saying there was no need of any money, the need is ...and she had started crying. Seeing her the little girl had also started bawling.

Hari had taken the child in his arms and comforted her. What else could he have done? He was quite at a loss. How would this distressing problem be resolved?

Both of them were quiet. Jasbir wanted to talk bout many things but he couldn't bring himself to. He was afraid that Hari would feel hurt. He might even start crying. He had a great desire to tell him how deeply Operation Blue Star [the storming of the Golden Temple by troops] had affected him. His mind had been in turmoil, he was tormented like a wounded poisonous snake. Then he had an insatiable desire to start spewing the venom which filled his whole system. He thirsted for vengeance but he kept quiet, hissing inwardly. He stared at Hari.

Hari wanted to ask Jasbir if he had killed anyone. But that would be like asking a brahmachari about his love life even if he should have transgressed slightly just once. He started wondering how Jasbir had become a terrorist.

Hari recalled that they had once visited the home of one of their Comrade's father, who was a wealthy landlord. In the sitting room there were many trophies – mounted heads of deer, their glassy eyes fixed on the visitors. Seeing them Jasbir had become agitated. He had said in the presence of the elderly Sardar, "This room looks like a butchery. What is so heroic about killing these innocent animals? Hunting a tiger is something else...." Jasbir could not bear to be under the gaze of those lifeless eyes and in a very short while he took his leave and left the place.... Which Jasbir was that? And what about the Jasbir who was so pained when he saw, as they were walking together, that a fire had been lit close to the roots of a laburnum tree? Lit probably by the same people who chopped off the tops of trees so that the branches did not interfere with the electric wires. The person who had once dreamt about communism and the rule of the proletariat and then switched to dreaming about the rule of the Khalsa was yet another Jasbir. The Jasbir who had started speaking with a forked tongue, saying one thing to Hari and another to others, the Jasbir who imagined that independence and freedom lay through the barrel of a gun. But instead of upholding Mao's little Red Book, he had turned to the saying of the Gurus for inspiration and guidance.

"Bhain....!" The swearword formed in his mouth but quickly retreated. It was a word that he had no compunction in using when talking with Jasbir earlier. He wasn't quite sure why he stopped. Was it because of Jasbir, or himself, or merely the circumstances in which they found themselves now face to face with each other? He looked carefully again at Jasbir' face. He felt that it wasn't Jasbir at all. It was a statue that resembled Jasbir, a demonic ghost, a ghost whose very existence spreads terror in those around and makes their blood run cold. He looked again at Jasbir, the terrorist, but there nothing of the sort could be seen on his face. There were tears in his eyes and his breathing was laboured.

In Jasbir's mind there was a vivid incident which was clamouring to get out.... One day, he wanted to tell Hari, when he was going to his village from a tiny railway station, walking along he had remembered Hari. For a moment he had imagined they were both walking together. But then Hari's absence hit him and the tears welled up in his eyes. He could not understand why he had wanted to cry. Now that he was actually with him why did he not have that same feeling? He said nothing about this to Hari but merely asked instead, "How frightened are you, Hari?"

"As much as the other Hindus. Or as much as the clean-shaven Sikh boys." Hari wanted to tell him that whenever he returns home late from the factory if he sees a young Sikh on a motor cycle, or a scooter, moped or even a cycle coming from behind, he feels faint. Recently he had allowed his beard to grow quite long. And if he were returning at night, he would wear a saffron turban.... One night the street light wasn't working. Seeing him this way, standing in front of the door, his family got a terrible fright. When anyone knocks, before opening the door they peer through the chinks.... That day, when they saw the turban they almost panicked even though he had told them that he wore a turban at night, and they had even seen him in it.... Others on the street used to get scared too.... Hari did tell him, and then tried to laugh it off. But Jasbir became very serious. "Hari, you don't believe in any religion. So why don't you grow your hair and become a Sikh? I mean at least look like a Sikh."

Hari could not make out whether Jasbir suggested this to save his friend's life, or whether he was making a play to recruit him in his effort to establish the state of Khalistan in the Punjab. Or else whether he sincerely believed that there would be no place for Hindus in Punjab, at least not to live in dignity but only as second class citizens just as the Jews lived with the Christians. If somebody spat on a Jew's face, the Jew merely wiped it with his handkerchief and continued on his journey. Jasbir believed that Khalistan would become a reality and he did not want Hari to live like that.

Hari felt entangled in his own thoughts and to escape he asked: "It must have been very uncomfortable to live underground?"

"Yes. It was."

"Did you ever come face to face with death?"

"Yes, but not much.... Death can happen anytime, anywhere. It has been my constant companion. That is why I am not afraid of it.... But I feel it now, sitting with you, inside in the house. When a person enters the security of the house, he begins to fear it."

"Have you had any narrow escapes?" Hari asked and looked closely at Jasbir's face.

Jasbir didn't answer. He relived those great moments when a person confronts death, when the choice is to kill the enemy or in the process to become a martyr himself. He wanted desperately to strike at the enemy's abdomen, split it open with a chopper, scoop out the entrails and scatter them on the ground or riddle his body with gunshot till it looked like a sieve.... Then it seemed as though it might be possible that their flags would fly atop all fortifications - the slain enemy was merely an obstacle in the path of this objective. When the Naxalite movement was at its height he had been arrested for supporting it. His deeply felt blood lust – whether by disembowelling or shooting – had had no outlet.

In order to hide his heart's secret Jasbir raised his knee and put his hand on the bandage.

Hari wanted to know if there is a difference between an accidental killing of a passerby and a deliberately chosen target such as a person on the hit list. The words formed themselves into sentences in his mind and remained there in a tangle. Instead he asked, "Is the leg paining?"

"No. There's just a mild itch," Jasbir replied as he removed his hand from his leg. Then he sat up, leaning against the wall.

Hari took out a packet of cigarettes but then changed his mind and returned it to his pocket.

Jasbir smiled and said, "Smoke. I know that without this you won't be able to talk."

Hari remembered that whenever he went to Jasbir's house, Jasbir would bring the ashtray and place it next to him. But the person sitting in front of him was not the same Jasbir.... God knows how many innocent people he has killed.... Hari moved his chair back a little and lit a cigarette. He looked at Jasbir gratefully. Jasbir found that the deep dislike he had for such people, specially those who smoked, lingered. But somehow he did not feel it for Hari. His heart overflowed with great love for him. He wanted to call his sister-in-law up. He wanted to have both the children sit beside him. He wanted to hold them in his lap and caress them. He would ask his bhabi how she was. Did she still have the pain in her stomach from which she used to suffer? Thinking about this his eyes filled with tears. He looked here and there, blinking, so they would dry up.

Hari had told his wife all about Jasbir but had not said anything to the children. The little boy had once asked why Jasbir Uncle didn't come to the house any more. He had merely said, "He is not well. He has gone to his village." The child had thrown a tantrum and insisted that he wanted to go to the village too, Hari had a hard time making excuses.

How Jasbir loved that little boy! He used to affectionately call him his Little Monkey. Whenever Jasbir visited, he would sit in his lap. He would eat with him. And Jasbir would feed him with the same spoon that he ate with.... Thinking about this Hari was overcome with emotion and found himself asking: "Don't you want to meet your Bandar?"

Jasbir put his arm across his eyes, covering them. Hari felt sheepish at his lack of tact. After a strained silence Hari tried to change the mood and asked cheerfully:

"Jasbir, do you remember our friend, Padma, the Revolutionary-turned-Comrade? You used to go red in the face when you got into a heated argument with her! She used to win the debate on exactly this point. Well, she has married an American and gone to live in America. She is now employed in a broadcasting company. That is how she serves her compatriots!"

Jasbir moved his bag from behind him and looked at Hari. Rubbing his eyes with a corner of his turban he thought: Is he having a dig at me? Then, very calmly, he said with great confidence: "A little while ago I resolved to forget my past, all that I have done. Friendships, relations, everything. Only then is it possible to mould the world according to your ideals.... But over the last few days I have begun to think it isn't possible to break all links. And yet I feel suffocated by the unbearable burden of my own hatred and anger. Let it be... The clock can't be turned back, it's best not to talk about these things now." Both of them fell silent. For a long time they could not speak. To escape the silence Hari busied himself with looking for ticks in Daboo's ears and killing them. And Jasbir moved his bag aside and stretched out full length. Hari was consumed with curiosity, he wanted to pull the bag towards him and see what was in it! But he couldn't even ask. Then Jasbir covered his eyes with his arm.

He seems unhappy, Hari thought. Perhaps he is thinking about his family. He was casting about for some other topic of conversation when there was a knock on the outer door. He signalled to Jasbir not to get up and went downstairs.

He opened the door and found the warden of the neighbourhood, Chaudhri Ram Saran, standing there. He thanked his stars it was not the police. The Chaudhri had come to inform him about the meeting of the Peacekeeping Committee.

Hari went up and told Jasbir. But the fear still lingered. Jasbir began to suspect that somebody may have seen him entering the house and informed the Chaudhri. Was it possible that Hari himself...? Or had the Chaudhri perhaps ....?

As it started to get dark that fear settled in Hari's mind. He wondered if the Chaudhri had any suspicions... perhaps Jasbir had opened the window and the Chaudhri had seen him. As far as Jasbir was concerned the Chaudhri was a bloody Hindu. Exactly what he hated. As he was mulling over these thoughts another fear settled in. What if Jasbir expected to spend the night here... Then what would he do? The house could be raided at any time! He began to wish that Jasbir would go, that would be best. In the face of death or starvation all affection evaporated. But he could say none of this. What he did say was: "Let us have dinner. I can get mah di dal from the dhaba if you like."

"No. Don't take the trouble to go anywhere." Having said so Jasbir felt that it had been prompted by a lack of trust in Hari. The way he had asked seemed different. Hari too did not like the way the abrupt No sounded. Did Jasbir think that Hari would betray him for the sake of the bounty? How could he think such a thought? Both of them were feeling upset. Then, to defuse the situation, Jasbir himself raised the point. "Just imagine! The government has offered a reward of Rs 10,000 for me!" And he laughed.

With the thought of how venality can drive a wedge in friendship still rankling in his mind, Hari went downstairs.

He brought dinner up, served in two thalis. It felt strange to Hari when they started eating. They had never eaten separately like this before.

When they had finished eating Hari took out the gur which he had also brought up wrapped in a piece of paper. Jasbir remarked, his face softening, "Old habits die hard. You still like eating gur!"

"But this doesn't compare with the gur you used to bring for us from the village. And those delicious sesame sweets which your mother used to send for me...." And both of them laughed.

After Jasbir had washed his hands, he started tying his turban saying, "I must go now." If he had spoken this way two years earlier Hari would have responded, "Oh yes? Daboo!" he would have said, "Catch the thief!" Or he would have begged him to stay longer, just another fifteen minutes. Or he would have said, "Let me finish my cigarette." Or they may have sung together:

"O! Friend-in-a-hurry! Spend a few more moments here...." He said none of these things now. Instead he heaved a sigh of relief even as he went through the motions and asked: "Where will you go in the night? Stay here."

"No. It is not right for me to stay here." Jasbir said as he opened the window and looked out. The street light was not on. He wrapped the sheet around his shoulders, covering his face. Before going down the stairs he asked Hari to go and see if it was safe to go into the lane.

Hari went down to find his wife standing in the courtyard looking pale and frightened. Fearfully, and softly, she asked: "Tell me the truth. Who is he?"

"He is a class fellow from Khanna.... He is ready to go now."

"Why are you lying? I heard you calling him Jasbir...."

"Yes. Yes. But he is not that Jasbir. He is someone else."

"Then why is he going at night? The times are so bad, moreover there is no bus at this hour...." She was on the verge of crying. Hari could not make out whether she wanted to send Jasbir away or hide him for the night.

"He has some relatives here. He'll go there," Hari said looking for a way out of the predicament. Then he opened the door and went out.

His wife stole up the stairs quietly. She stood by the door and peeped in. Jasbir was sitting on the bed. Daboo was biting his dangling legs in play and Jasbir, holding Daboo's ears, was rocking his head back and forth.

When he saw his bhabhi, Jasbir let go Daboo's ears and pushed him away. He stood up but was not able to hide his face nor greet her with Sat Sri Akal. She turned away and went down the stairs, feeling faint. Hari came in and gave Jasbir the green signal. Jasbir went down quickly, pulled the sheet over his face, and crossed the small courtyard. He stood in the doorway and looked around. Then, turning to look back at Hari, he said hesitantly: "Since the day before yesterday I have been trying to contact you to tell you something. Be careful. For the next seven days don't do night duty. And don't let the children go out!" He walked away quickly, limping, till he rounded the corner.

Hari bolted the door securely, and going into his room, sat down.

When he had gone to bed and lay there thinking, his wife came to him and spoke close to his ear: "What was the harm in telling me the truth?"

"Are you mad? He must be dead by now! Don't bother me, let me sleep."

He turned around and shut his eyes. He tried to sleep but sleep did not come.

He was worried about the wound.

WHO DID THEY MURDER?

Tauquir Chugtai

Yashodara's voice fell on my ears. She is our neighbour. She was entreating Gautama to return home. "For my sake and for the sake of your son come back. Why are you begging for alms from door to door? You are disgracing us all. Your father is the king of this state, and you a beggar…."

"The world is full of suffering, Yashodara! Neighbour kills neighbour. The ambitious want to destroy the homes of others, burn their fields. People live surrounded by disease and distress. I cannot bear to see all this. I have renounced this world full of sorrow; I have renounced matters of state, and also you….

"With the message of hope and trust, happiness and peace I am going to a neighbouring state. I hear that the inhabitants there are enmeshed in suffering from starvation, war, misery, and disease…"

Kis da Katal. Translated by Tara Meenakshi Sekhri

That was only three days ago. Yes. Only three days ago the yogi was alive and well. I saw him myself, he was telling Yashodara:

"People in this world are very unhappy, but they themselves are responsible for their own misery. Just see what is happening. The Sakiyas have made a bomb which, if it explodes, will wipe out the entire Kauliya clan. All vegetation will be burned to ashes, and there will be no future generations to continue the race. Following the example of the Sakiyas, the Kauliyas too have made a bomb and in no time at all both sides have stockpiles. It is a good thing that the enmity between these two sides has not reached flashpoint. So far, occasionally tension mounts but there is only a minor flare up somewhere or other.

"Just the other day a woman came to me carrying in her arms the dead body of her son and she said: 'Restore this corpse to life.'

"I asked her, 'How did your son die?'

"She replied, 'Between our clan of the Sakiyas and the neighbouring Kauliya clan a war has been going on about the ownership of a hill which actually belongs to neither of them. It is the home of the people who live there, but both these clans are claiming it as their own. In the course of the war for ownership people get wounded or killed every day. Today my son died. He was my only son! Breathe life into him....'

"I told the woman, 'Go to the next town and bring from there a handful of mustard seeds, from a house where no one has died.' The woman searched in every house but she found none which had not experienced death. She quietly returned and had nothing to say. Then I explained to her: 'Every living creature has to die. But not in the way these young men of the Sakiyas and Kauliyas are perishing. Death is the destiny of every person. Even after death there is no escape. But it is neither necessary nor right to go to war, or inflict pain on others, or to kill.'

The woman, some say his stepmother, Krisha Gautami, then said to him: "Just as you have created a group of bhikkhus there is need to bring women into the fold too."

And Gautama agreed and said to her: "Due to this constant fighting there are fewer men than women and it is all the fault of the men. War affects women the most. In the progress and development of life and society women are every bit as important and capable as men."

The prince of Kapilavastu, the one who left the Princess Yashodara and his sleeping son Rahul to wander in the wild woods, that Gautama was alive and well three days ago.

He was not a prophet, nor an avatar who promulgated any religion. He was the prince who renounced all desires, the prince who renounced his kingdom, who stepped out of his own class to go and live among the common people, the prince who wandered from place to place in his search for enlightenment. It is said that women, wealth and land are the compelling needs of human beings. Many people struggle to acquire these things, through fair means or foul, for the greater part of their lives. Gautama not only renounced his wife, wealth, and his kingdom but his newly born son as well. For him, to attain the Truth was the greatest need, the most important thing in life.

Yes. It is only three days ago that he, safe and sound, passed through our neighbourhood. He wasn't alone. There was a whole group of people with him also in search of Truth. They went from door to door, knocking. Whatever each one received in alms and charity, they shared among themselves and ate. They all looked quite alike. Bare heads, bare feet, their bodies covered with skimpy saffron-coloured cloth. I asked Gautama:

"Baba! Why do you wear these wooden slippers instead of leather shoes? Don't your feet hurt?"

His parched lips quivered as he spoke softly. "The reason for wearing these wooden slippers is that when other creatures – insects and ants, or snakes and scorpions – hear the sound they make, they can move out of harm's way. It enables them to escape being crushed underfoot by me."

"Why do you look so sorrowful and tired?"

"The world is full of sorrow," Gautama answered. "Is anyone happy here? He alone can be happy who performs good deeds, he who does not cause pain and suffering for others. I am going to the neighbouring state where I have heard the people are suffering from hunger, distress, and disease."

And he proceeded towards that state with the message of happiness, peace and contentment.

He saw there that every citizen wore around his neck, instead of garlands of flowers, or carried instead of books, a kind of a sling which they called a Kalashnikov. Everywhere there was the stench of gunpowder and the sound of explosions. The people moaned and groaned, unhappy and hungry. Many of them had fled to other countries, the rest had died. Those who were alive were worse off than the dead. Continual fighting had left them maimed, some had lost a leg, or a hand, others an eye. Gautama asked a passerby:

"Brother! What has happened? Why is your country so desolate? No child, no woman, no young person can be seen. Even if there are any, it seems as though they don't exist. Why are you quarrelling among yourselves? Stop this war mongering. Why don't you wage war against hunger, distress and disease?"

"It seems that you are a newcomer to our country. Perhaps you don't know that only those who follow our religion can live here. It seems to me that you belong to some other religion...?"

"I have no religion, nor enmity towards anyone. All religions preach the message of goodness. I have seen that the life of humans is divided into four parts. Hunger, old age, sickness and death. A human being is nothing more than this. Anyone who comes to know this finds himself. He realises the Truth, and there can be no religion greater than the Truth."

Having heard only so much that man raised a great commotion. In no time at all a crowd of collected and somebody asked: "What's the matter? Who is this wise man in saffron robes?

Why are you bothering him?"

"He is some yogi from the neighbouring kingdom come to pervert us with his fancy words of widsom. He thinks we are fools!"

"Leave him alone! He has uttered nothing bad. What he says is right," another commented.

"You belong to our faith and yet you want to mislead us?" Yet another spoke up.

"It is not a question of religion but of the Truth," Gautama insisted.

But no body listened to him. They dragged him instead to a huge hill. Then there was a loud explosion and when the dust settled Gautama's limbs could be seen scattered all over.

Yet just three days ago that yogi prince was alive and well. The radiance of Truth lit up his face. That Gautama, whom hunger, isolation and the wilderness did not touch, nor did the passage of centuries in the darkness of historical oblivion kill, that Gautama was murdered by a few bloodthirsty fanatics in the neighbouring country.

I have heard that in that country Gautama was the last remaining symbol of peace and happiness which provided its inhabitants the only anchor for any faith in humanity, any reason to trust. Now who will ever be able to trust those unfortunate people who call the act of killing innocent people a reason to hope for reward in a divine hereafter.

They say that Gautama has been killed. But they don't know… they don't know that Gautama can never be slain….

Gautama existed, he will live on.

Then whom did they murder?

Wretched, unfortunate people! Look for the answer in your own hearts…

III

THE TANTRIK'S PROMISE

K S Duggal

Parents, sister, brother, friends, relatives, her community – everyone, the whole world – was upset and angry with Menaka. Yet she had not deserted him. Mehboob! Well, the very name means 'beloved'.

'How can anybody ever turn away from one's lover?' she would muse in her heart and would pay no attention to what people said.

Much hue and cry it created. Much noise. But Menaka did not budge from her stand. She did exactly what she wanted. When everybody had shut their doors to them, they left for a distant, strange city where they went to the court and got married. A civil marriage.

Menaka said to herself that it was a mere formality. When they had first met, they were drawn to each other instantly.

Jogian de kanaan vich kach diyan mundran.
Translated by Satjit Wadva

That was their marriage. With the very first glance she had given herself to him. She was his, heart and soul.

By day, no peace. At night, no calm.

Some said his complexion was dusky and dark. Well! So what? Menaka would have sacrificed her own fair complexion a million times for his sake.

Some others told her that he was a foreigner. Those days Palestinians had neither home nor shelter. "One day he will desert you and leave," they said.

Menaka herself was working. She had a government job and didn't need either home or shelter. Wherever she was posted, government accommodation awaited her.

"Dear girl," others cautioned her, "you are a Saraswat brahmin and your lover is an orthodox muslim! The Palestinians have been involved in clashes with the Jews for years and years. Day in and day out they are at each other's throats. Every day there is a new issue.... Neither are the Jews defeated, nor do the Palestinians withdraw. Those people are indeed rude and crude....

Being in love with a young man from that country, it seems she has fallen in love with Palestine itself! But their race is forced to wander from pillar to post. They are dispossessed of their own country. Homeless! Now in Lebanon, now Thailand, now Tunisia, and now Egypt! Now here, and now there. People pitiably pushed around. What a wonderful physique! Moulded of steel yet they were being baked and scorched and burnt. Such people? They are ready to do, or die!

Their leader Yassar Arafat is so handsome! Menaka kept his photograph safely in her wallet like a good luck charm. Whenever she opened her vanity bag to touch up her makeup, she would steal a look at the picture. Some even teased her that she seemed to be more in love with Mehboob's leader than with him!

Certainly, Menaka would firmly reply. "Yassar will rehabilitate each and every Palestinian in his land. He will achieve a state and win justice for his homeless race. The Gaza Strip, the West Bank, and Palestine which the Jews have occupied. Well, might is right whatever the cause at stake. Millions of Palestinians have been ousted from their country. They are neither here nor there, the poor homeless refugees!" Her Mehboob was one of them.

And some would remind her that they were no more than terrorists. Anarchists! They hijacked aeroplanes! They threw bombs! How could such people be trusted?

Menaka would dodge the subject lightheartedly. "Yes! Someone has hijacked me too!"

She got herself transferred to Guwahati. Far away. Far away from her hometown and her own people. Out of sight, out of mind.

In Guwahati she had an isolated lonely house. There was no one to peep, no one to pester her. Nobody had the time to worry about strangers. Such a big city! The kind of city where parents met their children only on Sundays or at festivals, and no one had time for neighbours.

They had been here for quite some time but Menaka had made no effort to make friends. She didn't even have any acquaintances. She and her refugee lover Mehboob! It seemed to her that their self-imposed solitude was delicious and she would sometimes murmur softly: "It's an unending honeymoon…." She went to her office but kept her distance from her colleagues. She had no desire to answer any questions.

'Bibi, you are a Hindu. He is a Muslim.'

'You are an Indian and he is a Palestinian!'

'You have a fair skin….'

'He has a wheatish and tanned complexion!'

As it is she had managed to get away from her family and surroundings with such difficulty. She didn't want to encourage curiosity. With no questions asked, she didn't need to answer any, nor tell any lies!

It is a kind of intoxication to be able to do exactly what one wants. Menaka was in a state of drunken bliss. After all, she thought, she had not committed any crime. She had only loved. She had happily accepted the consequences, good or bad, of her own actions.

She had left her parents, siblings, relatives and friends. Crossed the country to settle in an unfamiliar city. It mattered little to her.

So Menaka had thought. For a while she did not miss anyone. But parental ties are not so easily abandoned as she was to discover contrary to what she had thought. It was over a year now and no one had tried to communicate with her. She had heard that her mother had not stopped cursing her and wishing her ill. "Perverse wretch." "Husband-devouring dragon." "Ogress." And whatever else came to her mind. It is inconceivable that any mother should say such dreadful things to her own child.

Menaka, thousands of miles from home, felt the vitriolic fumes of her mother's fury scorching her all through the day, both herself and her husband. Earlier she had felt it vaguely, but now for some time she had felt it strongly. It was as though she was being baked. As though long tongues of those accursed flames of hatred were leaping towards her, pouncing on her, ready to engulf her.

Then exactly that came to pass. Mehboob fell ill. There was no particular ailment, yet he was ill. He began to feel unwell, low and out of sorts. He lost his appetite. He lost all interest in dressing properly and stopped going out. Menaka continued to go to work; it provided some distraction for her while Mehboob stayed at home. He was wasting away, day by day, despite being under treatment. The doctors advised one test after another and Menaka scrupulously had them carried out but to no avail. Blood tests, sputum test, now this and now that. All kinds of pathological investigations were done and they showed nothing was wrong. Yet he continued to deteriorate, going steadily downhill.

When the doctors could do nothing more someone suggested to Menaka, "Why don't you go to Kamakshi's temple? It is on Neelachal, not far from Guwahati." In this temple the presiding deity is Sati, Lord Shiva's first wife, with her beloved Lord. The legend is that Sati ended her life by jumping into the fire of the havan because her husband had been insulted. Shiva almost lost his mind. He picked up the burnt body of his wife and carried it on his shoulders in a frenzy of grief. Lord Vishnu took pity on him and with his chakra he cut the body into many pieces, which fell in various places as a demented Shiva roamed the mountains. One piece fell here, on Neelachal Parbat, the blue mountain – her genitals. Of the hundred and eight temples built in memory of Sati all over the country, Kamakshi Devi's temple is one. It is vital and significant for ardent lovers.

Temple of love where Sati is in loving union with her Lord, Shiva, oblivious of the world! The old Vedic name of Guwahati is Prajapati Pura. Menaka was shocked to know that the locality in which she lived was known as the Place of the Ancients. The women there were known to practice the art of black magic. They could cast a spell on a person transforming him into a tame lamb and tie him to a peg in the courtyard. That is how this part of the country came to be called Kamarup.

Menakshi was still undecided about visiting the temple when her well-wishers, those who had suggested the trip to Kamakshi's shrine, put her in touch with a panda. The panda wore a tilak on his forehead, a white turban on his head and an angrakha over his shoulder, worn over the coat which he wore with a dhoti. He spoke pristine Hindi and had a practical conversational fluency in English. In fact Menaka followed his spoken English more easily than she could his difficult Hindi. It was not possible to enter the temple of Kamakshi without such a guide. Every day there were long queues at the temple, from morning till evening, of people wishing to get darshan of the deity. It didn't matter if it was burning hot or freezing cold, the queues were unending.

Pande ji seemed to be a cultured gentleman. What Menaka liked most about him was that he did not ask too many unnecessary questions. Without hesitation she gave him whatever amount of money he asked for towards the darshan of the deity. She felt that in such matters bargaining would be in bad taste. She wanted, more than anything else, that Mehboob should get well somehow or other, effortlessly as the result of a miraculous or magical cure. She was prepared to pay any price for it. As it is he was getting worse day by day. It was painful to see him. He had become just a bundle of bones. Sunken eyes. Drops of perspiration on his brow all the time. His limbs limp and lanky, his lips dry and cracked. His voice, when he spoke, seemed to come as a faint echo from the depths of a well. How long could anyone live in such a state?

In a day or two, Pande ji made all the arrangements for Menaka's puja. He bought all the items which would be necessary.

Kamakshi temple is located on top of a hill in the suburbs of Guwahati. There are more ways than one to approach it – east, west, north and south. The priests would decide which was the proper way to reach the deity according to the need and convenience of the devotees. Menaka was directed to take the northern approach. It was a detour, but so what? She was not walking like the other devotees – they had hired a taxi for the yatra.

The taxi arrived at Menaka's gate at the appointed hour on Tuesday. Pande ji, wearing clean white clothes, emerged from it exuding the fragrance of sandalwood paste and incense. The previous night her husband had been very ill and Menaka couldn't decide whether she should go, leaving him behind all alone, or not. She considered the fact that he was already getting the best treatment and medicines, and yet he was no better. In her heart she was convinced that he was under some evil spell. He had been perfectly fine and healthy. Someone must certainly have done what is known as Tona. Now none other than Devi Kamakshi could help. They had tried all the remedies. Only the puja remained to be performed, it was the last hope. Everyone had assured her that this yatra and puja at Kamakshi's shrine would completely cure Mehboob. People claimed to have witnessed the impossible happening.

Because Pande ji had already fixed the time of darshan, Menaka got into the taxi though half-heartedly, reluctant to leave Mehboob.

In the taxi, Pande ji talked as if to himself. "Guwahati is mentioned in the Ramayana and Mahabharata. We are going to the Kamakshi temple from the northern gate. Those who go through this gate attain nirvana, their wishes are granted. Those who go through the western gate get material wealth. Those who go through the eastern gate get prestige and position. But those who enter through the southern gate are doomed. They may even die!"

When she heard of death, Menaka felt her heart flutter, missing a beat.

"Mahashakti is worshipped in three forms," Pande ji continued his monologue. "These three states are the divine, the animal and the valiant. The divine state is the best and most luminous. The worshipper of the divine is pure and pious. His sins have been absolved. For him there is no difference between virtue and vice. He attains this through knowledge, gyan. Taking the sword of knowledge in hand, he reaches this state. In the second state, the animal state, the devotee is caught in the grip of doubt, hatred, fear, shame and so on – all the animal traits. Such emotions keep the person in bondage. The third state is for the brave. In this state the devotee rises above the animal state and does whatever he likes, disregarding all moral values. He eats meat, drinks alcohol, has sex."

A small pause. "Of all the mutths in India, Kamakshi temple is the only holy place where Mahashakti is worshipped in all its three forms," Pande ji was saying. "Why only three? Here Mahashakti appears in all her ten forms."

Pande ji was still talking spontaneously when the taxi reached the top of the hill, turned into a courtyard and stopped under a neem tree. Menaka was thus deprived of more knowledge from Pande ji about Mahashakti's ten terrible forms.

Getting out of the taxi, the first thing Pande ji did was to quickly open the boot. A little lamb jumped out of it. Menaka remembered it was to be sacrificed. It was evident from Menaka's ochre sari and blouse that she had come for a puja of Mahashakti. One of the bystanders came forward and held the lamb while Pande ji got busy getting the puja items from the taxi. It seemed that the people sitting there were familiar with Pande ji. Menaka looked up at the temple. It was overflowing with pilgrims. There was a very long queue. This would not finish before night.

First of all flowers had to be offered at the subhag kund. Here, too, people stood shoulder to shoulder.

She was not anxious because she had come with Pande ji. Apparently he had fixed everything in advance. Leaving the main gate he took Menaka towards the right. There were people there too, but not so many. Devotees sa- about singing devotional prayers. Some listened to the discourses of the pandas. All hands were folded. All eyes closed. Everybody was engrossed in prayer and deep faith.

Pande ji walked purposefully to the right carrying all the puja things, and Menaka walked beside him. It seemed that he was expected. People smiled in welcome, respectfully. But Menaka, in her heart, asked the Devi's forgiveness for entering the temple from the side door on the power of money.

And then a room, and another room, and yet another room. As they proceeded the darkness increased. Then a narrow passage, and some stairs. Lamps of pure ghee lit the place filling the air with intoxicating incense.

Here they could see the crowds coming from the main gate of the Kamakshi temple inching forward singing the praises of the Goddess. The organisers stood everywhere. Pande ji was talking in gestures with everyone, or occasionally whispering.

They reached the inner cave, the sacrosanct shrine. In the light of the ghee lamps a large stone was visible, covered with a golden crown and flowers. In front of it was a trough through which water from a natural spring flowed. And around it were statues of Ganesh and other gods and goddesses, wearing garlands. Mahashakti was the stone rock covered with gold and flowers. That's all. The devotees who had come in the queue were made to stop to allow Menaka to do her puja. She offered the things she had brought with her, uttered the mantras she had learnt by heart, and draped garlands on the shila and the devi-devtas. The priest blessed her profusely praying for the fulfilment of all her wishes. The priest was happy, and Pande ji was happy but Menaka's state of mind remained the same. The prayer was over. Before turning back Menaka once again bowed her head before the deity. Once again she thanked the head priest who picked up a garland from the shila and put it around her neck.

Menaka should have been pleased. Her puja had been completed without any hindrance. She had received a garland of flowers as prasad. And prayers had been offered so her wishes would be granted. Yet she was seized by a sudden sense of unease.

Menaka was returning after offering prayers to the highest deity in the temple but she could not shake off the depression she felt in her mind. She tried again and again but she was not successful.

In the meantime the taxi stopped at her doorstep. She opened the gate quickly, crossed the verandah and the courtyard and entered Mehboob's room. Pande ji was still collecting the left over bits and pieces from the taxi. As she stepped into the bedroom, she screamed. Her husband lay there lifeless. His head had fallen sideways off the pillow, the eyes were upturned, and a dribble of dried spittle marked the side of his mouth. His face was pale. And then a fly came and settled on his nose.

Just then Pande ji entered breathlessly. He looked at Mehboob and said, "He can't die! He is not dead. This can't happen after Mahashakti's puja! This is just an optical illusion." Pande ji looked at Menaka and repeated, "He cannot die! He is not dead!" Fixing his eyes on Menaka's face he said it once, twice, thrice. Again and again. And Menaka fell, like a stone, into his arms.

When Menaka came to, it was already dark. The door was closed and Pande ji was repeating some mantra continuously. He had bolted the door from the inside. The only sound audible was the sound of the continuous jap as though it was a charm, nothing else. Sitting on the sofa she listened to the hum of the unbroken rhythm. She couldn't make out if it was in Sanskrit or in Assamese. A never-ending humming, the sound of flies buzzing.

Night had fallen. There was darkness all around. Pande ji had not lit a lamp in her husband's room nor did she have the strength to get up and switch on the light. There was just the sound.

The darkness deepened. Then dizziness. She felt as though she was falling into a deep abyss weightlessly. She fainted again, falling on the sofa like a bundle of dirty clothes. The night passed in unconsciousness. Dawn was breaking when Pande ji woke her. She opened her eyes to see the Tantrik staring fixedly at her face. "He cannot die. He is not dead," he was saying with the same faith. "Mahashakti Kamakshi will have to return him." And he put a garland of fresh flowers around Menaka's neck.

A soft fragrance of jasmine. Where had the garland of fresh jasmine come from? The priest's garland of yesterday had withered long since. Crushed and trampled. Menaka stared at the glowing countenance of Pande ji who had kept awake the whole night. "He cannot die. He is not dead," he kept repeating confidently.

If he was not dead, and if he couldn't die, then there was no question of his burial. Nor was it necessary to inform people.

Pande ji's repeated assurances of "He cannot die. He is not dead" resounded in Menaka's ears. She was now convinced that what was being said to her was right. Everything else was wrong.

And so Menaka was enslaved by Pande ji. She would do exactly what he told her to do. And accept whatever he said.

Mehboob lay covered from head to toe in his bedroom. It was the third day. Pande ji chanted mantras day and night. The prayers were continuous. And the fragrance of incense hung heavy.

Menaka thought more than once: 'If he was really dead then how could the corpse remain as it is for three days without getting decomposed?' His room was in the same state. But it was throbbing with the hum of the mantras as though the sound itself was alive. There was a soft fragrance, the same that she had felt at the innermost holy shrine as she stood near the water flowing from the yoni at the temple. It was the scent of the burning ghee lamps, of the consecrated puja items, of the incense

She remembered when her friend's father had died, many years ago, and they had to wait for a dear relative to come, how many things they had to do to preserve the dead body for twenty-four hours. Blocks of ice underneath and all around. She didn't have to do anything. Pande ji had just said: "He cannot die. He is not dead!", and there he was, lying in his bed covered from head to toe. The recitation of mantras and prayers continued. Lots of flowers had been bought. Lots of more prayer offerings. The bedroom was shrouded in incense smoke all through the day; the fragrance felt as though she was passing by a Shivalya.

Then Pande ji took her again to the Kamakshi temple. The house was left as it was, Mehboob lying in bed as though he was asleep. The medicines remained on the table beside him. He could take the prescribed medicine at the right time. It was the fourth day.

This time they did not go to the shrine. The taxi stopped in front of one of the many houses built near the temple. They were expected. As soon as they reached there was a bustle of activity in the house. The head of the family, who looked like a priest, left the house saying, "The girl has gone to school. I'll go and get her."

Meanwhile, all the prayer material that Pande ji had brought in the taxi was being brought into the house. Red and yellow flowers, butter, milk, sindhoor, platters of sweetmeats, laung-supari, silken clothes, a tray of real pearls and lots of other things. Even toys for children.

They didn't have to wait long. The priest reappeared, holding a little girl by her hand. She was about seven years old. Delicate. Extremely beautiful, her thick dark hair falling down to her waist. She held a piece of khadi in her other hand.

When she came both Menaka and Pande ji got up in respect. She spread her cloth but before she could sit down on it Menaka offered her a handful of silver coins as instructed by Pande ji. This was symbolic of a silver seat.

Oh! How lovely she was! Fair complexioned, sharp features, and the dark brown eyes of a doe. Delicate. Silent, as though she couldn't speak. Such an innocent look! Menaka couldn't take her eyes off her.

The first thing was to wash the girl's feet. Menaka, herself barefoot, did so, pouring a lot of water and then wiped them dry with a towel as Pande ji instructed. Now Menaka looked at her as the beauty of the three worlds. She meditated on her as the queen of the earth, the sky and the underworld, of heaven, earth and hell. This is how she was welcomed. She was Saraswati. She was Jagdamba whom the whole word worshipped. Pande ji kept reciting mantras and Menaka repeated them after him.

Next they worshipped her body; her head, her bosom, every part of her. For each there was a separate mantra. First Pande ji, and then Menaka after him, recited them.

After that the girl was worshipped as mother and wife. Her feet were washed again and annointed with sandalwood paste. Aarti was done with flowers and incense. The fragrant smoke of incense started spreading and the lamps of ghee twinkled. Then the girl was offered food. Menaka fed her with her own hands, putting rasogullas and sandesh into her mouth, one after the other. Next, Menaka adorned her with ornaments and finally put a tilak on her forehead. This way the girl became Nav-Durga – the mother of all incarnations, the mother of Brahma, Vishnu, Mahesh. Having worshipped her thus, they left.

It was evening when they returned from Kamakshi after the puja. Menaka's house was as silent as when they had left it. Mehboob lying in bed, covered from head to toe. The ghee lamps burning as before. The fragrance of incense and the smoke filled the room.

"He is not dead. He cannot die." Pande ji kept reminding her. And she trusted him completely.

But then why didn't Mehboob remove that sheet and pull her towards him as he always did. He would either pull her towards him or come closer to her. Menaka lay in bed and waited for him.

Her mind insisted that Pande ji couldn't be wrong. Pande ji can never be wrong. And she had even worshipped the girl! He will open his eyes, if not today then tomorrow, or the day after as Pande ji had told her. Only his night had become a little long.

Pande ji had given her books to read. The methods and techniques of Tantra made her hair stand on end. As she thought about the dimensions of Tantra she started perspiring.

"First Devi will have to descend into his form. Then the Devi's symbol will have to be made of his brows, his cheeks, his lips, his breast, his navel, and below, to the accompaniment of the recitation of the mantras. Then with her permission, his male and female bodies will have to be made identical. The jap will be louder and louder. When the music reaches a crescendo, at that moment, focusing attention on Mahashakti, ejaculate. In this whole act there should be no desire, no longing, no wish. This is a method, a prayer."

She read on: "Kali's devotee has to go naked to the cremation ground, hair let loose. First he has to offer the flowers of a wild plant (Calotopis procera) soaked in semen. The hair and nails of the beloved have to be sacrificed in the havan kund...." And on: "The van margi has no need to bathe, brush his teeth, or keep the body clean. All this can be done mentally, and should be considered done. The Seeker must have a rosary of teeth around his neck and a skull in his hand. It is important to make a corpse the seat. And even more important than that is that the Seeker must have sex with a woman of low caste before going to the cremation ground. After having sex, he must kiss her vagina."

Menaka was amazed to see that philosophers like Sir John Woodroffe had translated sutras of this kind into English. And spiritually evolved people like Swami Vimalananda had explained them.

The next day Pande ji gave Menaka the Mahamrityanjya mantra. She had to repeat it one crore times to conquer death, to attain liberation. The Siddha can grant life to anyone. He can kill anyone he wants to kill.

Menaka started repeating the Mahamrityanjya mantra day and night. One day, two days. And she thought she would not be able to continue. Pande ji was so nice. He was doing so much for her but she would never be able to manage to repeat it a crore times. Her tongue was tired, her lips dry. She felt she had high fever and that her head would burst. Her body was wracked with pain. She felt walls of darkness rise before her eyes swaying this way and that.

Seeing her condition Pande ji said, "There is another way."

"But it should not be long." Menaka sounded like a weary traveller.

"Of course. It is a sadhana of just one night. But you will have to do everything alone, all by yourself. I cannot be included in it."

Menaka was ready. She would suffer any torture for one night. For one night she would even die if only she could get her Mehboob back.

As luck would have it, it was the night of no moon. Pitch dark. It was difficult to see one's own hand. The heat was suffocating. Somewhere an owl screeched and far away a dog howled. But Menaka was not at all frightened. She could only hear Pande ji's words: "He is not dead. He cannot die" again and again. He was such a great scholar. He had such discipline. And he had studied so many books!

All alone, a bag in hand, Menaka was moving fast. Tonight was her night of union. Never before had she done what she had been told to do now. But she would do it. What can't a man do if he really and truly wants to do it. Then Mehboob would get well. Tonight was her first night. Pande ji couldn't be wrong! Why would he mislead her? The man was an angel! It is so rare to come across such a person. He had stayed beside her for so many days. Day and night he had assured her: "He isn't dead.

He cannot die!" More than them even the followers of Kamarup are great. They can transform you into a lamb and tie you to a peg. They can tame even the wildest person and make him as gentle as a lamb.

As these thoughts went through Menaka's head she started reciting the beej mantra given to her by Pande ji. She became aware of an image floating before her. A naked woman. Tall. Blood on her breasts. She was standing on a snow-white blanket, a skull in her left hand. Her open mouth dripped blood. She wore a janeyu of snakes.

Not frightened in the least, Menaka continued to walk fast. Pande ji had told her that she would need to focus her attention on one point. Only one thought. One goal. One wish. One target. One attainment. Tonight was the night of union. Tonight was her first night.

Pande ji was a Raj Yogi. It was said that he had attained the eight maha siddhis. He could never be wrong. Hadn't he said, "He isn't dead. He cannot die."?

Pande ji had the Mahamrityanjya mantra. But this mantra can be a curse also. Surely not his! His mantra cannot be cursed. She thought of it and started reciting it. In one voice, in one rhythm she recited it firmly as she proceeded headlong towards her destination. This is how kama, artha, dharma and moksha are attained. While reciting the mantra her kundalini could awaken. It was said that Pande ji's kundalini had already been activated.

"The mantra is the only remedy," had been Pande ji's verdict. There are two thousand Pandas associated with the Kamakshi temple. And these two thousand priests remain in the service of Mahashakti.

At times Menaka felt that Pande ji was walking by her side. Like a shadow. She was surprised but not at all fearful. The very presence of Pande ji allayed all her fears.

"Pande ji, Pande ji!" She caught herself saying this and wondered why she was saying "Pande ji, Pande ji" all the time, whatever she was doing. It was as though she had forgotten Mehboob.

"Because he is dead," came a voice from within.

No! He was to be brought back to life. Tonight! Tonight was the night of the miracle. The miraculous night.

Engrossed in these thoughts Menaka reached a ruin near the cremation ground. In this deserted place was a neglected statue of Shiva. She had been instructed to worship this idol.

First quarter worship of Shiva. Second quarter perform karam-kand at the cremation ground. Third quarter back in bed. Fourth quarter union with Mehboob. That is how Pande ji had planned her night. Her night of union.

There were ruins everywhere. Bats and foxes. Scorpions and snakes. Stumbling at every step, she would save herself here but knock into something else there slipping and missing a foothold. Menaka was surprised but she was not at all scared. Perhaps that was the result of the herbal drink Pande ji had given her before she started. As time passed she felt the chill of the night; she felt every fibre of her body tingle as though she was intoxicated. But she charged forward, like a lioness, the puja items in her shoulder bag, given to her by Pande ji.

She saw in front of her, in the corner, Shiva's neglected statue which lay not quite upright. She did as she had been instructed. She was to bathe the idol with wine which she was carrying in the bag. Then, removing all her clothes, she was to sit in front of the statue, totally naked, and recite the mantra a hundred times. She had a choice here. He had left it to her: she could either recite the mantra or dance before the idol. Menaka did the japa of the beej mantra. She then put on her clothes and started moving towards the burning ghat.

It was just as Pande ji had chalked out for her. About ten feet away from the neem tree on the right of the cremation ground a corpse was burning. For a split second Menaka thought of jumping onto the pyre and immolating herself like Sati. Then she felt ashamed. What was she thinking? This was the night of the meeting! Kamakshi was returning her Mehboob to her. Pande ji had promised that. He couldn't be wrong! He had spiritual powers. He had said, "He isn't dead. He cannot die!"

Menaka went down to the river to bathe. This is what Pande ji had said: "She will bathe on the bank of the river, wash her hair, and then, completely naked, she will come up to the pyre of the burning corpse with a pan of river water and cook rice on it. When the rice is cooked, she will sit there and eat it. She will then go around the burning corpse four times. Relieved, she will wear her clothes again. On returning home she will go to bed with her Mehboob, just as she had been doing ever since she married him."

And then.... Then....

"He is not dead. He cannot die." The words resounded in Menaka's ears. She had finished bathing in the river. As she climbed up the pyre, the words echoed. "He is not dead. He cannot die." She put the rice to boil right on the skull. "He is not dead. He cannot die," Pande ji's words reverberated in her head when she strained the rice water from the boiled rice, and, as instructed, shared the rice with the corpse.

"He is not dead. He cannot die," the refrain continued as though someone was reminding her with every breath. Menaka completed the entire karam-kand without a hitch and returned home to lie down with her Mehboob.

How tired she was! She had not slept at all and the night was far gone. It was an ink black moonless night. Pitch dark. She felt a sort of relief when she lay down in bed. As if she had reached her goal. She had bathed the idol of Shiva in wine. She had bathed herself. She had washed her hair. In the cremation ground, she had put the pan right on the skull and boiled the rice just as Pande ji had told her to do. And then she had fed the corpse, morsel by morsel, taking one bite herself and offering one to the corpse. And then, turning the pan upside down, she had circumambulated the pyre four times.

Now, lying on the bed, all she had to do was wait. With this thought in mind Menaka began to doze. Her eyelids felt heavy. But how could she sleep? This was her first night.... Against her will sleep was descending on her, as though draping every part of her body. Her eyes were closing....

"He is not dead. He cannot die." The words were like music.

Who was singing? "He is not dead. He cannot die." There were many voices, men and women. It was a chorus – and they were singing and dancing. The voices rose and fell, sometimes the women's voices soared to a higher pitch, and sometimes the men's. Sometimes the men and women sang softly, together, murmuring "He is not dead. He cannot die."

Menaka felt that the wine with which she had bathed Shiva's idol was flowing in her body. She felt intoxicated and her body was so light. She was falling – lower and lower and lower into an abyss. The darkness was deepening.

And Menaka felt a hand move. It came out from the sheet next to her and crept closer and closer. Yes, Yes. It was Mehboob's hand, his arm. There was the ring that Menaka had given him. Oh! Where was this hand going…?

How soft! What a gentle hand! So sweet and delicate. How is it she had not noticed this before? Not felt it before? She felt drunk with the touch of this hand. She was going mad, wild with desire. Every part of her body responded to that touch, resonated to it. The touch became an embrace, lips met lips and her whole body dissolved into an involuntary quivering….

It was broad daylight when Menaka awoke. She was lying in Pande ji's arms. When she opened her eyes and looked at his face she felt it was Mehboob's face. To relive and relish her rapture, she closed her eyes again.

It is true there is magic in the country of Kamarup.

AND THE RIVER FLOWED ON ...

Amrita Pritam

Once, long ago, something happened – it flowed in the waters of the river until it came to a stop at the banks of a long distant epoch, where, in a dense forest, Ved Vyas was absorbed in deep meditation....

When he emerged from his deeply meditative state he found, standing before him, Rani Satyavati looking sad but divinely beautiful.

Bowing, like the leaves of a tree, he saluted her respectfully, saying: "My beautiful mother of many lifetimes! Why are you so sad today?"

She warmly embraced her saintly son, her heart full of maternal love and said: "You are descended from the line of Rishis, you cannot understand the pain of love and attachment. I learned to feel for an entire kingdom from Raja Santanu. For the prosperity and well-being of his kingdom I gave birth, from the same womb

---

Te nadi vehndi rahi. Translated by Jasjit Mansingh

that bore you, to two of his sons. One of these princes, my sons, was killed in battle, and the other died of an unknown fever leaving behind two distraught wives.

All the leaves of the tree seemed to tremble as they looked at Ved Vyas' saintly visage….

Rani Satyavati's thoughts flowed like the pure waves of the Ganga and she spoke: "Maharishi Parashar embraced me as though I was the Ganga. You are the pearl, the offspring, of the union of those waters. You sported by the riverside, in the water and on the banks. You ruled over the forest and its clearings, and over the wealth of its flowers. You cannot know the suffering of the pearl embedded in the crown."

Ved Vyas smiled like the greenness of a tree. "No, I don't know the sufferings of kingship, but I do know the torment of a mother's heart...."

Satyavati bloomed like an entwined creeper caressing the neck of a tree and she continued. "The pearl in the crown needs a throne, the throne needs an heir, and both my daughters-in-law are widowed. Today I have come to you seeking the boon of a son for each of them…."

Ved Vyas looked up into the tree spreading over him, and it seemed at though the entire tree was moved with joy as it gazed down on the earth which was covered with its seed.

The Rishi laughed. "This command of a mother, just as the imperative of the earth, will be fulfilled…."

Ved Vyas kept his word. He gave both Ambika and Ambalika the gift of a son each….

When the water of the river, gurgling like the chuckles of a child, began to flow again it passed through aeons of time till at last, in the time of Kalyug, the same incident was replayed at the banks of another time and place. There, where Baldev lived. It was an ordinary kind of home and life. Where, among the books on his table lay not only the Mahabharata but also Camus, and Kafka, and also Pasternak....

There, where his friend Kashi Nath stood before him like a leaf fallen from a tree, saying: "The boon that God has not been able to give me, nor any medicines from the vaid, that boon I have come to ask of you.... The gift of a son...."

There was no tree but the sound of the rustling of leaves in the wind filled Baldev's ears.

Kashi Nath was saying: "My wife's healthy body has been cursed because of the diseased body of her man.... My friend! Remove this curse. Just once...."

Baldev's entire body stiffened, just like the root of a tree.

Kashi Nath, as though he was a helpless leaf at the mercy of any gust of wind, fell at Baldev's feet. "This secret only I will know, you will know, and she.... Not another person, no one.... '

From within Baldev's body, which was still wooden and unmoving like the root of a tree, there arose a vision, a thought: 'Perhaps history demands this.... Perhaps I am a Ved Vyas, a rishi....'

And the same happening happened....

In a home where dejection held sway like windswept leaves now flowers bloomed....

Kashi Nath's wife gave birth to a son. Every one was overjoyed, all branches of the family. And when Baldev saw the child lying in his cradle, he looked carefully, he said not a word just as Ved Vyas had not.

"No! No. I am not Ved Vyas!" Baldev was woken from his sleep by the sound of his own voice which seemed like a scream.

On the small table next to his bed, the whisky left over from the previous night still lay. His hand shaking, he poured some into a glass and drank it in one shot, mumbling, "You were the son of a god, Ved Vyas! You were not a mere human being...."

He imagined that he was transported back centuries to that jungle and he wailed to the wilderness: "Mighty Rishi! You had the powers of meditation, deep meditation but all I have is dreams – many dreams...."

Baldev's words rose from his breast, and rising upwards bounced off the branches. "Look, you son of a sage! Look at me! See my Ambika.... You couldn't even recognise your Ambika the next day. But look! This is not my shadow, it is my Ambika...wherever I go, she follows me."

Then he laughed loudly. "Look, son of a sage! You don't have a shadow...it's true what people say – that gods don't cast shadows.... But man is cursed with a shadow.... Just look at my shadow, it is bigger than me!"

Then Baldev's voice struck the silence of eternity and he continued softly: "You came out of your meditation when Satyavati called you, but not when I call you.... Why don't you speak? You never picked up the child playing in Ambika's lap....

I have experienced that! I have held the child in my arms, caressed him, kissed him.... You don't know what it's like to let him go. It's like tearing out a bit of your own flesh...."

Baldev's whole body seemed soaked with the blood coursing through it. "You have never felt the passions of man, you son of a sage! Yes, a man has feelings – when he is deeply hurt.... And blood has a fragrance too. When a baby smiles, it triggers a warm feeling in one's own body, a sweet fragrance in the blood."

Then a pungent smell filled the veins of his forehead and he spoke as though blinded, half consciously. "The fragrance of my Ambika's body! It doesn't matter where she goes, I'll be able to find her... I feel her tremulous breath next to my shoulder, near my arm, it clings to my neck. Her breath is a treasure left in my care. And see! Within me too – I drank a deep draught from her lips...."

On Baldev's forehead one vein stood out as though forced by a sharp pang of pain. Biting his lower lip in agony he continued: "O Son of a sage! You knew only the act of giving. You didn't know how to receive.... You know nothing about the joy of accepting an offering.... I have come to know it. When I entered the folds of Ambika's body, I was in turn enfolded as though enclosed in a clenched fist – then my mind opened like the petals of a flower and when I re-emerged I was impregnated with her scent. That moment is not only about giving, it is also about receiving. I have experienced that supreme moment, O Son of a sage! You haven't.... It is not painful to give, it is exquisite torture to receive, and you, Royal Sage, have no experience of that bliss...."

There was peace all around, all around and as far as could be seen, and as far as Baldev could see in the future course of the remaining years of his life, there stretched an unending silence, a still darkness. Baldev, lying in the darkness, dissolved into it as a bit of denser darkness as though he had no separate discernible body but his lips moved as though the folds of darkness were undulating. "She came to get a spark of life from me, the same spark which lit the fire of life in me, yes, it blazed, but I didn't know – perhaps she also didn't know that to be quickened with life she too would have to suffer an ordeal by fire. The spark caught, the flames of passion enveloped her. She quivered in ecstasy merging with me just as though she couldn't bear a separate flame. And now she has joined the ashes of her passion with the ashes of mine. See, Royal Sage!"

Into the darkness of his face there arose a kind of shape – as though of a stone idol. Perhaps he himself had turned to stone with the passage of time, or perhaps he was still alive but still as a statue because he was so deep in meditation. Baldev waved an arm through the darkness as though to find the ground so he could touch his feet. Like the uncertain movement of his arm, his voice too was shaky. "I forgot, Royal Sage! Being merely human I tried to imitate you! I experienced it for just a moment, only one moment. It is as though I usurped your seat of meditation for that moment, but I can't do it.... You are still sitting in your jungle, unmoving but I, in my jungle, am lost.... I received not only the boon of giving but also the curse of receiving. I want my Ambika near me, and my son too.... See! I can look into the future as well as into the past – I can see as far back as the time Ambika was with me, holding me in her arms, and I was sprouting in her womb...."

Baldev, half conscious, slipped back into sleep and the stillness of the room heaved a sigh of relief.

The only movement was the fluttering of the pages of the books lying on the table caused by the breeze from the open window. They moved as though some particular portion of the *Mahabharata* had stood up to say something to Camus' *Outsider*. Or perhaps Pasternak's *Zhivago* had woken from his sleep to try and wrest from Maharishi Parashar the secret of Matsyagandha's transformation into the Yogin Gandha....

All of a sudden it was as though the quietude of the room was startled and looked towards Baldev in trepidation as he got up, agitatedly, from his bed saying, "What kind of a curse is this, Ved Vyas! Whenever I sleep, a burning desire takes hold of me – me and my Ambika – and when I am awake it all turns into a heap of ash, I have nothing. Tell me! When my child grows up how will he discover his lineage in that heap of ash?"

And the river flowed on, in the same way.... Only its waters saw, sorrowfully, that that incident had turned to ash which lay on the far bank....

THE POND OF MILK

Kulwant Singh Virk

Being first cousins, Lal and Dyal were very fond of each other. They farmed jointly too. Friendship between brothers creates a great impact in the village, specially because they were not really brothers. Such a union is very rare and they were considered to be a power to reckon with. Brothers are expected to stay united and these two, Lal and Dyal, were held up as an example in the village. The workers were easy to handle because they would obey them. They enjoyed walking in the streets of the village because they were respected and held in such high esteem.

Even without this unearned respect, their work in the fields was easy because they worked in unison. They ploughed the fields together. And if they employed one helper, then one of them would be free yet the work went on smoothly. A single person ploughing alone is very dull boring work, nor is it effective.

Dudh da chappar. Translated by Satjit Wadva

Alone the poor man is no better than an animal, and if he employs a labourer then it is not economical for him.

This joint farming allowed one of the cousins enough leisure which was the privilege of Dyal whose father was the older brother. Dyal was fair skinned, good looking and robustly built. In the mornings, before noon, he would work in the fields but in the afternoons he would invariably put on clean white clothes and saunter in the streets of the village or just hang around here and there. People enjoyed exchanging pleasantries with him and talking to him.

But all this enjoyment was possible only because Lal stayed back and toiled.

"Yesterday you didn't return from the village in the afternoon," Lal would complain occasionally. "The wheat field had to be fenced and you know how difficult it is for only two people to put up the fence."

"I just became lazy...," Dyal would say looking slightly sheepish. "The thanedar had come to the village so I decided to stay back and listen to him." And Lal would stop complaining.

Lal's wife often noticed Dyal loitering about in the house while Lal was busy in the fields. She would see Dyal's turban from over the common wall. Sometimes he would take his son to the carpenters and get them to make a toy cart for him. Sometimes he would go to the blacksmith to get the handle of the sickle fixed. Or he would go to the weavers to get the spinning wheel tightened. Her own odd jobs always remained pending.

Dyal's presence in the house, the sight of his turban and the sound of his voice, stirred strange desires in her heart. She wished for Lal to be home at this time so she could serve him a bowl of milk. She would give him pure white clothes to wear and go to the village. She would starch his turban as he dressed. But what was the point in giving him nice clean clothes to wear? After a week or ten days he would ask her to put them under his pillow and then wear them to the fields leaving his dirty ones behind. Soon these too would be soiled but he would continue to wear them for a few more days. If only Lal could also spend the evenings at home like Dyal!

When he came home at night she couldn't help saying: "You have got his helper, so the Sardar roams the streets while you slave with the soil!"

"What's wrong with roaming in the streets? He had gone because we had to ask for our turn to get water," Lal would explain trying to pour oil on troubled waters. "Sometimes the plough has to be repaired, or the rope has to be twisted, or a labourer has to be engaged on daily wages. There are hundreds of chores to be done in the village."

"If there are so many jobs to be done, then why don't you come sometimes? Why does *he* have to do all the chores in the village?"

"Okay, I'll come! Does it really matter? Usually he says, 'I'm going.' So I say, 'Fine. You go'."

Lal would often promise to come but he never did. He really didn't have much say in this matter. His routine was to get up by starlight, get the plough ready and go to the fields. Dyal would get up later, at dawn, get the buffalo out, put fodder for her and then milk her. He would bring enough fodder for the animals and then take them out for a little while. In the afternoon he would sit down to have a drink with a friend, or play cards, or listen to the news and try to make sense of it. Gradually the entire burden of farming came to rest on Lal's shoulders alone while Dyal was busy making friends and influencing people. That is how it happens in every partnership. One partner works more than the other. And as long as the former keeps quiet about it all goes well. But if resentment begins to pinch, then the partnership too starts to come apart.

One day, after the harvest, the blacksmith's boys were out collecting sheaves of wheat for their own stocks from the farmers. As it happened Lal was sitting in another jat's home when one of the boys came in to ask him for wheat. His companion already had his headload.

"From where did you get your wheat?" The jat asked the boy.

"We got it from Dyal's khalwada."

Lal's blood froze when he heard this. They had a common stock in the fields, but here it was being referred to as Dyal's! It seemed as though his own name was being erased from his property and possession even though he did all the work! He decided to separate. After the harvest of course, that would be the time to change....

As it is they already shared the crop. This time he divided the fodder also and they tied their buffaloes separately. One buffalo, which had calved recently but the calf died, was accustomed to being handled by Dyal. No one else could milk her. Lal wooed her. He fed her with salt in the gram, gave her flour to eat from his hands, offered her milk from his cupped hands, sprayed his breath full of milk into her nostrils, until he finally conquered her. Now she allowed him to milk her even though she remained very attached to Dyal; whenever she broke loose, she would seek him out or set out with his buffaloes.

The buffalo stayed loyal to Dyal, but Dyal and Lal started drifting apart. Since their fields were next to each other, very often the animals would break loose and enter the other's fields. Both parties accumulated many complaints against each other. On such occasions they would shout at each other and neither would relent. When Dyal's little calf spent the whole night in Lal's field of turnips, Dyal passed it off by saying: "I can't go myself and tie up the calf! These tiny animals get away somehow or other…."

The next day, Lal's mare wandered into Dyal's field of cotton. When he tried to chase her out she bolted, running through the field and her steel chain swinging from her halter decapitated the flowering heads of the crop. Lal defended himself: "The mare doesn't eat cotton. The plants were destroyed because she was agitated and frightened…. If you had allowed her to go quietly nothing would have happened." Dyal was furious. The turnips, after all, were only fodder while cotton was a cash crop! There was only one saving grace. Lal and Dyal had never come to blows.

Some days later it rained. Dyal had a room outside but Lal, who had not yet roofed anything, did not want to take shelter in Dyal's room. He found a dry spot under his shahtoot tree. So he wrapped his shawl around him and sat under the shahtoot for as long as it rained. This became the talk of the village. Herons had built their nests in his shahtoot and people said, "The herons bathed on the branches, and Lal bathed under them!"

After this rain it was understood that it was only a matter of time before a direct confrontation took place between Lal and Dyal. Some said that Dyal, who was the stronger of the two, would hit out. Others said that since Lal was more angry he would be the first to strike.

Lal's wife heard these comments and was frightened. She asked him, "I've heard that Dyal wants to pick a fight with you?"

"Does he want to die?" Lal shot back. "He won't dare to challenge me," he continued proudly.

To prove himself the better of the two, Lal crossed all limits one day. Before sowing wheat in his field Dyal wanted to spread a layer of straw. But the only access to the field was through Lal's field. Dyal thought that since that field was lying fallow there would be no harm in taking the bullock cart through it. But when Dyal brought his loaded cart, Lal was waiting. Standing on the fence, with a stick in his hand, he sent the bullock cart back.

At night when Lal told his wife about it, she was convinced that Dyal must be slightly scared of her husband. Dyal was discomfited and uncertain about his position. He felt extremely irritated, without any particular reason.

One evening, about dinner time, Lal was returning to the

village on his horse. On the way, Dyal and another person were sitting by the water channel on the outskirts of the village, drinking. They saw Lal, and Lal saw them. He could not avoid them and the horse had to slow down to cross the channel. Lal had nothing with him except his empty water vessel.

"Who is it?" Dyal asked in a stentorian drawl.

"It's me, Lal," Lal said firmly and then made encouraging sounds to let the horse drink water. It was as though he was actually saying to Dyal: "Come on! I'm waiting!" But nothing more happened and Lal continued on his way after his horse had finished.

At home he told his wife: "I had my lota ready.... I would have hit whoever came at me on the head. I tell you, mounted on a horse a man is worth four men! He can overpower anyone."

"Well done!" His wife said approvingly with a twinkle in her eyes. "I wouldn't expect anything less from my husband."

Lal was very pleased with himself. He was full of confidence, his steps were firm and there was a slight swagger as he walked about the house, and his heart overflowed with love for his children.

Then one night it drizzled a bit. Lal felt so relaxed that he did not get up to put fodder for the animals at dawn. The buffalo had broken loose from the peg which had become dislodged because the rain had softened the earth. She must have gone in search of fodder. Much later in the morning Lal brought her back from the street, put fodder for her, and sat down to milk her.

Her udder seemed very loose today as though she had already been milked. Now she was allowing herself to be milked for the sheer greed of more fodder. But who could have milked her? There was only one person who could milk her – Dyal! So, it was Dyal who had milked her...

All the teats were shrivelled and the udder flaccid.

He tried anyhow and got a mild trickle from one teat. What was he to do? What would he tell his wife? Dyal had been very foolish.... His wife knew perfectly well that other than Dyal no one else could milk the buffalo. And how could he remain quiet after Dyal had done this? It was possible that Lal would fight with him.... But if Dyal apologised he would be quite satisfied. Perhaps he would bang on his door with a stick, but both of Dyal's brothers-in-law had come and they would surely not let him come to the door. Lal kept caressing the buffalo's udder and pulling on the teats but they were absolutely dry. The last trickle had long gone.

Suddenly Lal had a brilliant idea. It is difficult to estimate spilt milk. Even a little bit appears to be quite a lot when it is spilt. If he upturned the lota he could tell his wife that the buffalo struck it with her hind leg.... As it is the whole place was wet with rain and there were small puddles here and there. He upturned the vessel.

"The damn buffalo went and spilled the milk!" He told his wife as he came in.

"Oh! No! How?"

"She just struck the lota with her foot and it turned over."

"Such a buffalo deserves to be beaten!" She said as she thought of the prospect of the whole day without even a drop of milk.

"Poor thing. Why beat her? A bee must have stung her and she reacted...."

She got up from near the hearth and went outside to see the scene of the crime. Everybody is interested in unusual circumstances – like a crashed aircraft, or a truck turned turtle, or, in this case, spilt milk.

"Oh! Yes! So much milk! There's a pond of milk here!" she said.

And Lal breathed easy.

Satisfied.

BHABI MORNI

Amrita Pritam

"O Jindo! Unfortunate soul! How are you going to spin these cotton wicks now?"

She had washed her cotton-like white hair with soapnut and as she squeezed the water out of the wick-like wisps she talked to herself. It was as though she was winding the very threads of her existence on the spinning wheel. "Who can stop time, or reverse destiny? Now that the fledglings can fly who knows on which tree they will perch, and what the future will bring?

She had made a nest in her own heart for the three boys. Hundreds of things had to be done for them. She had no time to rest yet she was never tired. The eldest had got married and gone away to work. The younger two had left for the city to pursue their studies. Because she sat idle, Jindo felt every joint in her body stiffening.

Translated by Tara Meenakshi Sekhri

"The years of black cotton passed well. How shall I now weave the white and grey?"

Thoughts that never surfaced in her youth now confronted her in old age like the pain in her knees as she remembered how her jet black hair had cascaded down her back, just like the exotic plumage of a peacock.

"O Sau! You gave me the name Morni! But the peahen has no plumage in her lot, no tail to spread like a fan before the world. Peahens merely shed fountains of tears and look down towards their ugly feet..." And her gaze slipped down to her own cracked heels.

Sau was her husband's brother. He was but a lad when he had seen her as a young bride embroidering a peacock with fine green thread on a white pillow cover. He had then called her Bhabi Morni. Coming from a humble plebian household, Jindo's soul had soared with Sau's implied appreciation and her needle worked effortlessly to create the most marvellous plumes. When she had finished the pillow cover she started embroidering a dupatta of the finest muslin from Chabbi choosing once again a peacock feather pattern rather than the usual mix of floral designs. Wearing this draped on her head she stepped lightly when she walked, resplendent as a peacock, and had soon became known as Bhabi Morni in the whole village.

Eventually, Sau got married. He fathered three sons in a row. Bhabi Morni had cuddled them, pampered them and fed them. Her own existence had gone fruitless. When some good old crone in the village would remark on it, tauntingly, she would seat the sons of Sau on her knees and feed them curd and sugar. And she would laugh: "No, Grandma! No regrets! Isn't it that a woman only fears that in old age when her knees fill with water, then ...? Eh? One has to eat triphala, isn't it?" Then, showering kisses on Sau's sons, she would croon: "Look at these! They are my three fruits, my triphala – Haradh, Baheda and Amla! Won't they treat me with compassion?"

"Just watch!" The other would say to give her solace. "In His abode justice might be delayed but it is never denied." But when her husband, the one who filled Bhabi Morni's courtyard with plumes and pleasures passed away, her own abode was filled with the gloom and darkness of sorrow, of a divine injustice.

A peahen sheds tears gazing endlessly at her own feet, but when a woman weeps she sheds tears waiting to see what Fate has in store for her. When her numbness wore off, that is what she mumbled to herself constantly as she went about her chores mechanically.

When sorrow descends, it goes down the chest of a woman and down the hands of a man. Sau worked himself to the bone ploughing and sowing his own fields as well as Bhabi Morni's. The vacuum God had created in her life could not be filled by another man, but Sau saw to it that she was not deprived of anything else.

'At least for the sake of the children she will light a fire in the hearth otherwise she will just eat stale musty food and neglect herself,' Sau thought. So, under some pretext or other, he would send his children to her house. Even otherwise there was but a wall separating their homes. Often the children would go to sleep on this side and wake up on the other. Their mother would carry them back while they were asleep or else Bhabi Morni herself would take them home, fast asleep, clasping them with their heads resting on her shoulders.

Sau's wife had to go, unexpectedly, to her maternal home at the death of her father. But it was as though she had gone for her own funeral. On the same night she had a severe pain in her chest, a writhing anguish, and she did not live to see the next day.

"Her pyre was beckoning her," people said – her wailing mother's relatives as well as her husband's relatives. That was how they mourned for her. But Sau had a fresh worry. What would become of his children? He knocked at Bhabi Morni's door saying: "These Haradh, Baheda and Amla of yours will get neglected. Take charge of them."

Then Bhabi Morni, her eyes moist with tears, pressed those children to her heart but she said: "Sau, I am obligated to you in many ways. I am indebted to you with every pore of my body. But who will stop tongues wagging in the world? Sau's face had fallen, like a spray of water on fire-baked bricks. The world as such was out of sight but Sau was right there, right in front of her eyes. Bhabi Morni, looking down at her feet, let the tears flow.

"So be it, my brother-in-law. My honour is in your hands. I shall not refuse to look after your sons." Though the partition remained, the two homes, despite the wall, became one. Bhabi Morni saw to it that the children did not miss their mother summer or winter. Her own hunger and thirst merged with their hunger and thirst.

Well, about a year and a half later the plaster of the wall which divided the two houses wore off during the rains. She made no effort to repair it. Then a kind of hollow formed somewhere along the wall. The children used to cross over through that. Gradually the entire wall collapsed. It was as though the wall had become an eyesore for itself and it disintegrated bit by bit.

By and by the boys grew taller than her shoulders. Very soon Bhabi Morni barely reached their shoulders. Sau had not taken sanyas from anyone but the villagers declared that he must certainly have been a yogi sanyasi in his last birth. His conduct in this life was that of a true saint.

"O Jindo! How will you spin out your life now?" Thoughts that had not crossed Bhabi Morni's mind for twenty years surfaced. Perhaps she had no time for such worries earlier but now that the three boys had gone to the city such thoughts started nagging her – whether she was resting or whether she was busy. Her heart was bereft, empty like a nest from which the birds have flown.

Deep in the desolation of her heart she saw her dilemma clearly. Just then she heard a knock at the outer door.

'May be the eldest one has come from town...' she thought as she got up. By the time she reached the outer door she had churned countless thoughts. 'O Obstinate one! I told you time and again to get married like sons should – tying a sehra on the forehead and then bringing the bride home. But no one knows what he did or didn't. He just wrote a letter to say that he was married! He brought her home for only one night... She seemed to be an Anglo-Indian, a Christian.... Well, that's the way he wanted it! ... Again, I repeatedly told him that when she reaches full term, he should bring her home. There, in the city, who would take care of her...? That's exactly what had happened.... She was so young...who knows if she looked after herself, what she ate or what she drank.... Within forty days of giving birth to a boy she went....! Today, it is just two months since she died... He is so impetuous, he couldn't even wait for six months. In the third month itself he wants to remarry...!'

But as she unbolted the door, standing there was not the eldest son from the city but Sau who had returned early.

"Are you feeling all right, Sau?" Bhabi Morni asked in alarm.

"I'm fine. It's just that I wanted to consult you about something....," Sau said as he entered.

"Is all well? Is there a letter from the eldest?" Bhabi Morni asked as she seated herself next to the foot of the string cot.

"In the old days the souls of fairies used to live in the bodies of parrots – half your soul too is with him and the other half is with the younger ones..." Sau looked as if he was deep in thought, yet he also seemed angry.

"How can that be? As far as they are concerned I might just as well be dead – it is such a long time since any of them visited...." Bhabi Morni protested.

"Aren't you glad to be free of them? You wrecked yourself working for them."

"And now that I am not, should I be idle and simply pickle myself?"

"Right then. Don't be idle! The eldest one has written to say he wants to get married! But his new companion is not willing to keep his child."

"O How terrible.... Whoever heard of such a thing? Turning away from one's own son...!"

"He writes to ask permission to leave his son with me."

Bhabi Morni was stunned. A gloom settled in her mind. Then she continued: "Sau you weren't so old when your wife died but you never thought of marrying again.... Just look at this! The boy couldn't even wait for four days...."

"It was different in my case," Sau said, sighing deeply.

"Why? How was it different? You were a hundred times better than any of your sons!

"Oh! Yes?" Sau laughed, but the sound got stuck in his throat. Finally he managed: "But you didn't tell me this then!"

"It is hardly something that can be said.... If you had indicated even once I would have arranged seven brides for you...." Bhabi Morni put her hand on the wooden edge of the charpai and levered herself up to sit on it.

"Never mind the seven brides.... You see, I had the presence of one person.... I was fulfilled and content with just that, so what need did I have to say anything...?" Sau answered looking intently at the blank wall in front of him.

"Hain? ....Oh! ....Heavens!" The realisation of what he had just said was like a flash of lightning passing through her cloud of white hair.

"Yes. My youth was not wasted," Sau reaffirmed, his face brightening.

"Well....Whatever is past is done....it was well spent. But now? In old age..." she mumbled and cut him off.

"Did I ever say it was not well spent? Remember when you once said – 'Oh Brother-in-law! My honour is in your hands!' Well. I have seen to that...." Sau's heart was at the point of bursting like rain-laden cloud.

Bhabi Morni looked at the ground for a long time, then she became resolute, like the earth itself. "Enough, Sau! What we did not think about all our lives.... What is the point of thinking of it now?

Sau was silent for a while, as he sucked at his palate with his tongue. Finally he spoke:

"Right! Tell me. What should we do about the boy?"

Bhabi Morni responded tartly. "What to do with the boy? Bring him home! Lying in his cot here, he will make it feel like a home again."

Sau got up and wrote a few lines on the postcard and once he was done he went to his usual corner, as he did everyday, and sat down to have a small drink.

Bhabi Morni, as she did everyday, put the daal on the chula to cook. While she was waiting, she felt something strange happen to her. A flame of warmth surged in her heart. She fed four bits of firewood into the earthen chula. Then she put the kadai, half filled with oil, on the fire. When the oil was hot she fried pakoras of finely cut onions. She took them to Sau, who was still sipping his daru, and left them next to him....

On the fifth day the eldest boy came from the city. He stayed for just the night. When he had dropped the four-month old baby, just like a kitten, in Bhabi Morni's lap and gone away, she had swallowed a handful of white cuminseeds and drawn the infant to her breast.

In the village they still talk about this – that for a whole year this grandson of Sau suckled at Bhabi Morni's breasts....

ON VACATION

Ajeet Cour

An oven-baked silence.

The sun, like an inverted arrow, seemed to pierce the bosom of the sky scorching everything. Like a burning oven.

It was so hot, so humid!

Such blazing heat that all around there was a deadened silence. Not even the sound of a sparrow chirruping. The birds were also exhausted, thirsty, and silent.

On one such fiercely hot afternoon, directly under a baking sky, working in one of those bare fields, was a man. An ordinary kind of man, a farmer. In an ordinary kind of field. And the village too was exactly like all other such ordinary villages. There was one semi pucca house constructed with lime mortar. The rest of the houses were all built of sun-baked mud.

Anyhow, at this moment he was outside the village, ploughing his field.

Chhutti. Translated by Jasjit Mansingh and Ajeet Cour

'Wah! What strange logic, O Creator of this Universe! How strange are your ways! Unless there is a long interlude of scorching sunshine the wheat doesn't ripen. While ploughing, large drops of sweat must fall onto the earth. Drops of human sweat as large as the grains of wheat. That is the law of all creation! You know, of course, because you made these laws. By the time the harvest is brought in, the sun glows red like red hot iron in a blazing furnace. Red? No, dear Mangal Singha, not just red! Bright, scorching, orange-crimson red.'

That is the way he talked to himself while he worked - addressing himself – 'Mangal Singha'. Saying, 'Well, we might as well go and have a bath, Mangal Singha!' Or, 'What's the point of bathing! The next minute you'll again be drenched in sweat and covered with dust. And then, Mangal Singha, we don't have to perform any holy puja!'

When his eldest son Kartar was killed he was prostrate with grief. He had been like a tree felled. Lying flat on the ground with dead arms stretched out. Dead! He felt as though he himself was a corpse lying on the bare earth.

Tongues wagged. Each person had a different explanation. Some said that the police had killed him. Others whispered that he had fallen out with the terrorists and they had finished him off. Yet others speculated it was an act of revenge because of some old enmity within the family. And some said that he was drunk; he got involved in a brawl in the market and his opponent killed him.

The police speculated that there must be another angle – it

must have been because of a romance gone wrong.

Finally, one day Mangal Singh pulled himself together. 'Come on, Mangal Singha. Kartar has gone now. Perhaps he had to pay a debt to me carried over from a past lifetime. Or he had to collect a debt from his mother and me! When the account was cleared, he went on his way. If you sit about helplessly who is going to feed the rest of the family? God? God is relaxing, Mangal Singha! Sleeping comfortably in his blue heaven. He is not coming to help you. Get up. And get moving!"

He did.

And he didn't stop.

They say wounds heal with time. Mangal Singh's wounds were not visible any more, but he knew they were there – just under the skin. The slightest scratch and the blood started flowing again. He tried to keep himself busy with all kinds of other thoughts, afraid of the phantom memory of his dead son. He reined in his mind constantly to block all remembrance of Kartar, and all voices coming from the black tunnel of memory.

It was the season to plough for the new crops. It was the time to upturn the earth and soften it. Hard work

But even when the work was not so demanding he would find one thing or another to do. He would tell himself: 'Mangal Singha! What is this mind? Only a restive horse! Pull the reins tight. That's all!'

Or he would say: 'Mangal Singha, what do you expect to get from God? He uproots from here, and replants there. Isn't that what Sain Bulleh Shah Fakir said?'

He had not really thought about God. Ever. He must be someone or other, Mangal Singh had resolved. Enjoying the heavens He created! Sleeping in carefree repose. Waking in the soft dew-drenched glow when the sky is washed clean and the sun begins to shine again and there, far away, the seven-coloured swing can be seen.

Bebe used to say that God makes the rainbow so He can swing on it.

Actually he didn't have much use for God, particularly after Kartar's death. 'If He does exist, there is terrible chaos in His accounts. Otherwise how could he kill a young lad who had not even seen the twenty-second spring of his life? Even a village patwari sometimes bungles the accounts, and that One, Mangal Singha, in his heaven must have a whole sky full of account books and ledgers! What can He do with everything brimming over? He must have lost control, Mangal Singha!

'That is, assuming He tries. Otherwise, what work does He have, Mangal Singha? To swing on the seven-coloured rainbows, sleep like a king on his soft bed of puffy white clouds, and stroll about in the blue skies? If he had to work the plough in the middle of this blazing afternoon, then the little sod would know what kind of a world he has created and how much credit it does him!'

While he was ploughing, and encouraging the bullocks with little tchch tchch sounds alternating with smacking kissing sounds, every now and then he looked towards the dusty path that came from the village. Yes, at this time of day, the path always 'came' from the village. In the evenings the same path 'went home' towards the village.

'Basant Kaur is taking a long time today to bring the food. I'm so thirsty it feels as though there is a thorny keekar growing in my throat. If I have water now my stomach, which is like a burning oven, will rumble like a thundercloud and simply vapourise it. Then I won't be able to eat anything! And then Basanti will make me feel guilty – "I've taken so much trouble..." she'll complain and sniffle.

Just then he became aware, that far, far away there was someone on the footpath, not in the direction of the village but on the other side. Coming from outside the village.

"Who can this be, Mangal Singha, walking in this burning heat?"

Isn't it strange...? Earlier when people saw anyone approaching from a distance they would be very curious. Curious and happy too, like children. They would want to know eagerly whom the person was going to visit in the village. Whose guest he was; whose Mama, Chacha, or brother? Or perhaps the visitor was from the paternal family of some young wife! It wouldn't matter whose guest he was. He would not have been allowed to proceed before acquaintance was made and he had been offered a refreshing drink.

How times have changed! Now the sight of a stranger strikes fear. Raw, naked terror! One human being is frightened of another. 'Mangal Singha! A lion is not frightened of another lion walking by even if it should be ten times stronger. But human beings...!'

Now the far-away outline of a human figure was acquiring some detail. A distant hazy picture was coming into focus.

The man was wearing old style jutthis on his feet, shabby and dust-laden. Every step raised a little puff of dust. Every time he took another step the dust followed, hugging his feet. It seemed as though he had walked a long distance. His footsteps were heavy, as though he was exhausted. There seemed to be an increasing weariness with each step.

His clothes - kurta pyjama - were covered with dust. A carelessly wrapped cloth around his head passed as a kind of turban.

And there was something on his shoulder too! A sort of a bundle. Perhaps he was a small-time trader, a salesman; the kind who buys some cloth, or bangles or groceries, from the city and then walks to nearby villages to sell his wares. Perhaps it was only a thick coarse cloth he carried to protect his head from the heat of the sun, and to wrap himself with at night.

His head was bowed as though he was measuring the miles he had walked. Or even his steps. He looked down towards his own footsteps and the dust he raised. In his hands there was a khoondi, a heavy stick that he seemed to be dragging along. His face was deeply creased. He was quite old. He appeared to be very weary and weathered by the woes of time.

Mangal Singh's first reaction was to say nothing and allow him to go on his way. 'Whoever it is, what do I care! These are bad times, Mangal Singha! Who knows who he might be! What if he has a gun, an AK 47, hidden in that cloth bundle? Don't acknowledge him, Mangal Singha. Be indifferent like people are these days, and let him pass.'

The old man came nearer, and standing on the boundary of the field, fixed his gaze on Mangal Singh.

The intensity of his gaze was such that Mangal Singh could not ignore him.

"Can I have some water?" He asked in a mild, deep voice, barely audible perhaps because of his exhaustion, or perhaps because of the dust choking his throat.

There was a round earthen pot of water, steadied on a square wooden frame, under the sheesham tree. Mangal Singh stopped ploughing. He unyoked the bullocks and unhitched the plough. Clucking at the bullocks he led them to the shade of the tree and said, "Walk across, Bapu ji. There is no shortage of water. Drink as much as you want."

'Let him quickly have his fill of water and go wherever he is headed,' Mangal Singh thought to himself.

Stepping through the soft ploughed earth the old man came into the shade of the tree. Mangal Singh filled the small brass bowl from the pot and offered it to him. It was then that he looked hard at the bundle that the old man was holding close to his chest.

Mangal Singh felt a terrible tightening in his innards. He had held the bag containing his son Kartar's mortal remains in exactly the same way when he went to Kartarpur Sahib to immerse the ashes. Who knows if the old man has also... and he felt his heart melting.

All of a sudden he felt speared by fear, the sharp point grazing his heart. 'Mangal Singha, there could also be explosives in the bag!'

He then tried to calm himself. 'Perhaps he also has a Basant Kaur who packed some food for his journey – she may have given him missi parathas to eat when he got hungry. And if she made missi parathas then there should also be mango pickle wrapped in them." And he smiled inwardly.

'O Mangal Singha! No one on earth can cook like Basant Kaur. Is there any other woman in the world who kneads the mixed wheat and gram flour with fresh butter for the parathas? And who puts chunks of spicy mango pickle to go with it?' He almost chuckled at the thought of Basant Kaur cooking parathas on the crackling firewood in the chullah.

'Never mind. If the old man wants to eat his food here, under the shade of the tree, then I'll give him lots of lassi which Basanti will be bringing. That will be something for him to remember us by!' Then cold logic took over.

'But Mangal Singha, what if he is not a Punjabi! Instead of missi rotis in his bundle he may just have roasted gram, or parched rice, or cooked rice, or who knows what else! I can't quite make out from his face where he is from. Well, what difference does it make to me...? But if he is from outside, why is he wandering around here in the villages of Punjab along these dusty roads where danger lurks even at high noon? There is nothing left here now.... Even the Bihari labourers are now deserting Punjab.... Nor does he look as though he is capable of doing any physical work. At his age he should be relaxing in his own home, sitting on a charpai in his own courtyard. This is no time for him to be roughing it out in a strange land being torn apart by violence.'

By this time Basant Kaur had put before him a round basket of rotis and a small pail of lassi. He didn't even know when she had come, or when she sat down next to him. She too was looking at the old man.

Mangal Singh split the onion with a sharp punch of his clenched fist. He took out the rotis, wrapped in an old worn out but freshly washed piece of white cloth. The aroma of the pickle escaped and was wafted in all directions.

He took two rotis, placed on them half the onion and a chunk of pickle, and held them out to the old man. The old man silently accepted them and gently breaking off bite-sized pieces began to eat.

The difficulty was that there was only one brass bowl, placed face down, on top of the earthen water pot in which he had served water to the old man earlier. Basant Kaur filled it with lassi and handed it to the old man. He drank from it – glug glug glug – till it was empty.

'A thirsty throat, Mangal Singha,' he chuckled to himself, 'is as vigorous in an old man as it is in a child.'

Then Basant Kaur washed out the bowl with a little bit of water and, filling it again with lassi, put it down in front of Mangal Singh. He too gulped it down at one go. To make sure that they didn't run short of lassi, Basant Kaur then filled the bowl with water from the pot and drank that.

While he was eating the old man did not look even once at either Mangal Singh or at Basant Kaur. She of course thought that he must be an acquaintance of her husband because when she had reached there both of them were sitting together under the shade of the tree.

When both the men had finished eating, Basant Kaur returned to the village.

The old man remained sitting under the tree, holding the bundle tightly close to his body, and looking down at the ground as though he were counting the ants walking in the packed earth.

It was Mangal Singh who broke the silence. "If you want to lie down shall I spread the sheet under the shade?"

The old man didn't reply and Mangal Singh took his silence for assent. He spread a thick sheet right there under the shade of the tree. The old man got up. He put that bundle down on the sheet very carefully and gently as though there was something in it which he feared might break. Then he stretched out, placing his head on the bundle, and shut his eyes.

'The poor man! He seems exhausted...,' thought Mangal Singh.

His first reaction was, 'Poor fellow! Let him sleep.' But then it suddenly occurred to him that there might be something dangerous in the old man's bundle. Perhaps bombs! That's why he placed it so carefully on the ground!

He couldn't help but ask, "Where have you come from, Bapu ji?"

The old man opened his eyes. His eyes held an age-old tiredness and despair. But even then there was a strange hypnotic power in them, a kind of luminous glow. Like the soft light from a lantern in a far away darkness.

In silence, for many moments, he looked at Mangal Singh with those sad eyes from which the tremulous glow continued to emanate.

"Where are you going?" Mangal Singh asked again.

"Nowhere."

"But a person who travels under the mid-day sun must surely be going somewhere!" Surprise and suspicion were both growing in Mangal Singh's mind.

"Nowhere in particular. I just set out. I was feeling restless so I set out on a journey."

"Journey to where?"

"Nowhere! Just.... I just had to leave and come away!" There was a tired resignation in his voice.

"What is your name, Respected One?"

"Name?"

"Yes. Name!"

"My name is God."

'Wandering in the sun, the old man has lost his mind, Mangal Singha!' Mangal Singh thought as he smirked under his moustache. But he asked with a straight face.

"God?"

"Yes. God."

"God. whose name is Wahe Guru?"

"Call me whatever you want. I am God."

"Then dear God, what are you doing in this dust filled godforsaken place?"

"Just!" He shrugged. "I got restless so I took some time off."

"You have to take time off? From whom? Who do you need to ask?"

"Myself. Who else!" The old man mumbled in a disheartened way. His voice was tired but crystal clear.

'God? How can this be, Mangal Singha! God who lives in comfort in the skies! The One who walks among the stars! The One who lights up the Sun and the Moon! He who enjoys the seven-coloured swings! This old man is pulling my leg!' All these thoughts rose like bubbles in Mangal Singh's mind, arising and dissolving.

It was as though God read Mangal Singh's mind. He said, "No, I am not fooling you. I really am God. I saw, and wondered why on earth I had created this world! Man devours man here. Such a thought never crossed my mind when I was creating the universe. I see now what chaos I created. How monstrous they have become, they whom I created in my own image! I couldn't bear my loneliness any longer. There is nothing more terrible than a depressed lonely person, and that goes for me too." Tears choked his voice. "Me! God!"

"But God if you saw that, you could have brought everyone to their senses with one strike of your staff. Why did you need to take leave?"

"No. I got tired. They take my name and proceed to kill each other. So I thought that if I take leave then perhaps they will stop murdering each other."

"Will this slaughter stop? Will this madness of destruction of humankind by man himself come to a halt?"

"Who knows!" God said, his words barely audible. And he sighed deeply.

'Poor man, he has lost hope. He has become terribly disillusioned,' thought Mangal Singh.

"As disillusioned as disillusioned can be! I'm so exhausted. Have you an extra bed at home? I'll sleep outside in your courtyard at night. At dawn I'll go away."

"But I still have work to do. I have to finish ploughing the field."

"Never mind, my good man! Do your work. I'm quite comfortable here under the shade of the sheesham tree. I'll take a nap and then we will go to your home."

Mangal Singh could not understand what was going on. He got up and took the bullocks to the little canal that trickled through the fields. They drank till their bellies were full. When they lifted their heads again it seemed as though their polished horns gleamed brighter in the sun. He then fed them and continued with his ploughing talking all the time with himself. He argued whether the stranger lying under the sheesham tree was merely a demented old man, ignored and humiliated by his young sons and his daughters-in-law, or whether he might actually be a terrorist. But can such an old man be a terrorist?

'Why not, Mangal Singha! He can be a messenger. A gun-ccarrier! A bomb carrier! He could be anyone.... But why do his eyes shine with such magnetic innocence? Why is it that I rather want to believe him?'

The sun had set. He unyoked the bullocks, put the plough across his shoulders and said to the old man: "We should go now. It will soon be dark. These days it is best to reach home before nightfall. The times are very bad."

So the old man slipped on his jutthis, flung the cloth over his shoulders, clasped the bundle close against his chest and started walking with Mangal Singh.

'O God, take care of me. If he is an informer or a terrorist, is it wise to take him home?' Mangal Singh was thinking. The times were bad. In such times people become suspicious and full of fear.

"Are you seeking protection from me? Are you asking me to keep you safe from terrorists and the police? I'm sorry. Now I'm not in a position to grant anything to anyone any more. I'm taking time out. I'm on vacation," the old man said.

'That's strange!' Mangal Singh thought, quite taken aback. 'How does he come to know what is in my mind?'

On seeing that same guest whom she had seen in the afternoon walk in, Basant Kaur, without a word, put in some more flour into the paraat and started kneading the dough. Happy and content to have a guest to look after and serve with hot food.

All of them had their dinner.

A bed was placed in the courtyard. A khes was spread on it.

The Old Man took off his jutthis, dusted them, and slipped them under the bed. Then, holding the bundle upright he patted it gently and put it at the head of the bed. He then lay down, placing his head gently on the bundle.

"If you won't take it amiss may I ask you something?" Mangal Singh said to him, softly.

"What?"

"What do you have in the bundle which you don't let go of for even a moment?"

At last a soft little smile settled on the old man's face. His eyes shone a bit brighter and his voice was like honey – sweet, soft and friendly.

"Not much. A handful of stars, a wisp of a cloud, the sound of birds chattering early in the morning, newly sprouted shoots, leaves of grass, a few dewdrops, about a cupped hand's worth of running water from streams and rivers, the first gurgling of an infant in a cradle. And some dreams. I thought I should save these at least."

He then shut his eyes, sort of snuggled into the bundle and went to sleep.

AUTHOR NOTES

Ajeet Cour has written 19 books of short stories and novellas which have been extensively translated in English, Polish, Russian, French, Bulgarian and Spanish. She has also translated several classics into Punjabi. She has won various national and international awards, including the Sahitya Akademi Award. She is the Founder chairperson of the Academy of Fine Arts and Literature and the Foundation of SAARC Writers and Literature.

Both her stories have been taken from *November Chaurasi*, Navyug Publishers, Delhi 1996.

Amrita Pritam has published over 75 books including novels, poetry, short stories and philosophical vignettes. She writes in Punjabi and Hindi. Her second autobiography, *Shadows of Words* (Macmillan 2001) is a voyage of the spirit. Her poetry takes precedence over all her other work. She has won innumerable honours and accolades, including the Sahitya Akademi Award, was awarded the Padma Shree and honorary doctorates from six Universities. She is a nominated member of the Rajya Sabha.

Both her stories have been taken from *Mitti di Zaat*, Nagmani Publishers, New Delhi 1993.

Baldev Singh, a comparatively young writer of Punjabi fiction, has written three novels, a collection of light essays, besides five collections of short stories and a number of one-act plays. He has received the Maxim Gorki Award; Bhai Mohan Singh Puruskar and the Nagmani Award. He lives in Moga, Punjab. His story has been taken from *Nagmani*, September 2001.

Buta Singh has written over 300 short stories and published four collections beside two novels, excelling in both genres. He explores the dark side of human nature and exposes human frailty through his finely etched characters. He is a master storyteller with great wisdom and understanding. He is a recipient of the Sahitya Akademi Award.

His story has been taken from *Pichle Dahake di Punjabi Kahanian*, Punjabi Akademi, Delhi 1993.

Jaswant Singh Virdi spent his career in teaching in schools and colleges and writes full time since he retired. He has published five collections of short stories, four novels, three plays and a collection of essays. His short story is taken from *Aalhineo digge bot*, Lahore Bookshop, Ludhiana, a compilation of Punjabi stories by Gurpreet Singh, 1998.

K S Duggal, scholar, poet, playwright, novelist and short story writer, has been prolific. Among his important literary awards are the Sahitya Akademi Award and the Soviet Land Nehru Award. He was conferred the Padma Bhushan in 1988 and nominated to the Rajya Sabha in 1997 in recognition of his contribution to Indian literature.

His short story is taken from *Pichle Dahake di Punjabi Kahanian*, Punjabi Akademi, Delhi 1993, of which he is the Editor.

Krishen Singh Dhodi is an aspiring writer, who did not persevere. His story, in its English translation, is taken from *Land of Five Rivers*, Jaico Books, 1997.

Kulwant Singh Virk, acknowledged to be a master of the art of the short story, is a link between the old and new masters of this genre. In many of his stories there is a satirical contrast between the sophisticated urban protagonist and the simple and honest way of life of the country dweller. With his writing the Punjabi short story enters a new phase of modernity.

Both his stories are taken from *Merian Sresht Kahanian*, Navyug Publishers, Delhi 1992.

Manmohan Singh Bawa, keenly interested in archaeology and anthropology, is an artist, cartographer, trekker besides being a writer. He has won an Indian national award from NCERT and is a recipient of the Punjabi Sahitya Sewa Samman from Punjabi Akademi, Delhi. His most recent book, *A Comprehensive Touring and Trekking Guide to the Indian Himalaya, including Sikkim and Bhutan*, is illustrated with his pen and ink sketches and maps.

Both his stories have been taken from his latest collection of short stories, *Nar Bali*, Chetna Publishers, Ludhiana 2000.

Mohinder Singh Sarna has been writing for more than five decades. His first collection of short stories was published by Sikh Publishing House in 1950. He writes in Punjabi (11 collections of short stories, 4 novels, 3 volumes of poetry) and in Hindi (3 collections of short stories, one novel) and his work has been prescribed in University syllabi. His concern is with humanity itself giving his stories a universal character. He writes of the dispossessed, the callous-hearted and exposes the hypocrisies of society in an increasingly militant world order. It is powerful writing which leaves a lasting impact on the reader. He has been honoured in Punjab as well as by the Punjabi Akademi, Delhi (Waris Shah Sanam) and the Sahitya Akademi.

His story is taken from *Merian Chonvi Kahania,* Navyug Publishers, Delhi 1993.

Prem Prakash, proficient in Urdu, has published seven collections of short stories, a novel and three volumes of selected short stories. He has been honoured by Punjab Sahit Academy, Chandigarh; GND University, Amritsar; Punjabi Akademi, Delhi; Punjabi Sahit Academy, Ludhiana and the Sahitya Akademi. He edits and publishes a literary magazine, *Lakeer*, in Punjabi.

His story is taken from *Pichle Dahake di Punjabi Kahanian*, Punjabi Akademi, Delhi 1993.

Raj Gill wrote for more than four decades with a great understanding of the politcal and spiritual dimension in the life of the Punjabi and its civilization. However, recognition came to him only with the publication of his novels, four in the space of less than two decades.

His story is taken from *Pichle Dahake di Punjabi Kahanian*, Punjabi Akademi, Delhi 1993.

Ramindra Ajit Singh took up writing late in life and has published two volumes of short stories. She is a devout Sikh, a student of the Granth Sahib, and has recorded shabad kirtan.

Her story is taken from *Kanki*, National Bookshop, Delhi, 2000.

Tauquir Chugtai lives in Karachi and writes in Punjabi. He is one of the youngest writers in this selection. He has a strong social conscience and is deeply concerned about the political misfortunes hounding the peoples of the subcontinent in the recent and continuing climate of terror and violence.

His story is taken from *Nagmani*, June 20(

Some Comments

"Good literature transcends man made barriers ... The 18 stories represent some of the most widely known names in modern Punjabi literature ... the writers who belong to different political ideologies give a glimpse of the character of Punjab's hardy people as they face the vicissitudes of troubled times. The collection gives to English readers a glimpse of the rich treasure of Punjabi literature."

Tribune on Sunday

"Discussions on the superiority/inferiority of vernacular literature ... the debate and consequent revival of interest in language literature couldn't have been more timely [at the ICCR Retreat, February 2002] for these translations of 18 Punjabi stories ... which cover Punjab from a historical and modern perspective."

Indian Express

"As the title suggests the past ... intrudes on the present so that along with stories dealing with life in the 20th century there are also counter-stories describing ancient legends, history, hallucinations and fantasies which also infiltrate the present. The little details of life in rural Punjab will engage even non-Punjabi readers. The writing is specific place, brilliantly evoking the colour and ambience of a landscape with an admirable economy of expression."

Biblio

"Even the most involved of postmodern narratives put up a show of being simply stories, while planting various devices to ensure that they aren't so simple after all ... In the case of this anthology the simplicity shines on the surface like the sweat on the face of the honest Punjabi peasant. What is below is not always simple. The stories are told in a manner which could be broadly described as factual, straightforwardly descriptive and narratologically uncomplicated.

Several of the stories are woman-centred. Whether deliberately or by accident, it is an exhilarating change. Women are projected here in many different facets, some being more well-etched than others. Buta Singh's 'Sardarni' is a portrait like someone from a 'comic epic in prose' genre. Mohinder Singh Sarna's 'Maa' is infused with a sense of powerful magic working through the mother, and 'Bhabi Morni' a story of subdued passion such that only Amrita Pritam can write.

In some stories the focus is on events – a massacre, a battle, the horrendous calamity of Partition rioting ... All these stories add up to the one grand narrative of Punjab – the narrative of its traumatic history, including terror, bloodshed, rape, barbarity as some of the underlying themes. It is perhaps to do justice to this all-encompassing narrative that many of the writers have adopted styles as flat as the Punjab plains ... solid and earthy, full of wisdom and devotion, whimsicality and humour, and the translations bring out these qualities well.

The quality of the printing is excellent, and Manmohan Bawa's sketches are pleasing. In this respect, the anthology does great service to Punjabi writing, because good presentation can certainly do its bit to accord this literature its rightful place among others when there are so many books jostling for attention."

Pushpinder Sayal, Prof Dept of English, Punjab University,
Chandigarh in *The Book Review*

"The translations seem to do justice to the original stories ... Punjabi literature is grateful for this effort ..."

Kahani Punjab

"It is by no means easy to translate from one language to another ... the translators have selected the right words and expressions in English which stay close to the original in Punjabi."

Shabad